Snow on Blueberry Mountain

by the same author

THE BLACK BUCCANEER
LONGSHANKS
RED HORSE HILL
AWAY TO SEA
LUMBERJACK
WHO RIDES IN THE DARK?
T-MODEL TOMMY
BOY WITH A PACK
CLEAR FOR ACTION!
BLUEBERRY MOUNTAIN
SHADOW IN THE PINES
THE SEA SNAKE
THE LONG TRAINS ROLL
JONATHAN GOES WEST
BEHIND THE RANGES
RIVER OF THE WOLVES
CEDAR'S BOY
WHALER 'ROUND THE HORN
BULLDOZER
THE FISH HAWK'S NEST
SPARKPLUG OF THE HORNETS
THE BUCKBOARD STRANGER
GUNS FOR THE SARATOGA
SABRE PILOT
EVERGLADES ADVENTURE
THE COMMODORE'S CUP
THE VOYAGE OF THE JAVELIN
WILD PONY ISLAND
BUFFALO AND BEAVER
SNOW ON BLUEBERRY MOUNTAIN
PHANTOM OF THE BLOCKADE
THE MUDDY ROAD TO GLORY
STRANGER ON BIG HICKORY
A BLOW FOR LIBERTY
TOPSAIL ISLAND TREASURE

Snow on Blueberry Mountain

Stephen W. Meader

Illustrated by Don Sibley

SOUTHERN SKIES

ISBN 978-1-931177- 78-8 cloth
ISBN 978-1-931177- 79-5 paperback

Library of Congress Catalog Card Number: 61-10112

SOUTHERN SKIES

LITTLE ROCK, ARKANSAS

www.southernskies.com

Dedication

The republication of this book is dedicated with love to Gary D. Edens---radio entrepreneur, hiker, trusted advisor, traveling buddy—by his great friend of 40 years, Jerry Atchley

Snow on Blueberry Mountain

Chapter 1

Mark Wilkins threw back the quilts and crawled out into the cold darkness. He did it quietly, not wanting to wake his two younger brothers, asleep in the other bed. In the little room it must have been close to freezing. He pulled on his clothes in a hurry, trying to keep his teeth from chattering.

In the kitchen his mother was up and had a fire going in the big wood-burning range. "You're early," she told him with a smile. "Figured you'd be lying late on a Saturday morning."

"Not today," he replied. "It's the last day o' deer season. Buck Evans an' I haven't done any hunting yet, an' we thought we'd try to get us some venison."

Mrs. Wilkins nodded. "We could use meat," she agreed. "Better be careful in the woods, though. Sometimes it seems as if more hunters get shot than deer."

She was a jolly, sturdy woman, not given to worrying. Mark was glad of that, for he knew his mother didn't lead an easy life. Less than a year earlier she had been left a widow with a brood of six youngsters to raise. And though he himself was nearing seventeen and almost a man grown, she had insisted that he finish high school. Outside of what he could earn in the summer, their main support came from his older sister, Bess, who taught in Crow Ridge Consolidated School.

Mark finished his oatmeal and flapjacks, bundled himself into his Mackinaw, and went out to milk the cow and feed the pigs. The first light of dawn was beginning to strike the eastern slope of Blueberry Mountain. There was only an inch of snow on the ground, but the air felt heavy, as if a storm might be on the way. That was fine, he thought. Tonight he'd better get down his skis and wax them.

With the early chores finished, he put on his bright red hunting cap, took the scarred Winchester from the wall, and set off down the road. It was less than a mile to Buck's place. The state highway skirted the foot of the mountain, with woods along both sides. Now, in the early morning, he could hear the chatter of jays and the softer cheeping of chickadees and grosbeaks among the trees. Twice he met cars with hunters in them, heading over toward Bear Creek.

Buck was up and waiting for him. He was a tall, rugged young man in his middle twenties, tanned from outdoor work.

"Had your breakfast?" he asked with a grin. "I wouldn't want you to give out on me 'fore we get over the ridge."

"Don't worry," Mark answered tartly. "I'll outlast you in the woods, afoot or on skis, any day in the year."

They were friends of long standing, and exchanges like that were common between them. Eight or nine years earlier, when Mark had been known as "little Buddy Wilkins," he had helped Buck find the big wild blueberries he had crossed with cultivated Jersey bushes to create the famous "Pocono Sky-Blues." Now that Evans had made a success of blueberry growing, Mark worked for him regularly in the summer months.

They set off up the hillside, following a little-used wood road. Old Tige, the coon dog, went with them. A trifle stiff in the joints now, he still loved hunting above all things, and he could be trusted not to bark and frighten the game.

Buck had his new rifle, a handsome and expensive one, and he glanced with some amusement at the old Winchester cradled in Mark's arm. The younger hunter caught his look.

"O.K.," he said with a laugh. "She's not very pretty, but I've kept her clean, an' she'll still shoot straight."

For two hours they climbed steadily. The thin snow was undisturbed except for rabbit and squirrel tracks, and Tige paid no attention to those. He seemed to know without being told that they were after something bigger. Just after they crossed the shoulder of the mountain, the old hound ran ahead a few paces and nosed eagerly at something in the snow. Mark hurried forward to look.

"Fresh tracks," he announced in a low voice. "Looks like three of 'em—a buck an' two does."

"Good," said his companion. "Let Tige trail 'em. We'd better separate a little an' see if either one of us can get a shot at the buck. Too bad there's no open season on antlerless deer this year."

The dog needed no urging. He followed the trail at a businesslike trot, while his master moved off to the right and Mark to the left. They were experienced woodsmen. There was no crackle of broken twigs as they threaded through the brush.

The way led downhill now. Soon Mark felt moisture under his boots and knew they were near the swampy area that lay in a hollow of the mountain. Off to his right he could catch glimpses of his friend's scarlet hunting jacket, forty or fifty yards away. Between them, Tige was still pushing on.

A light breeze seemed to be blowing in Mark's face. To make sure he held up a wetted finger. He was right. They were approaching the deer upwind. Then he saw the old dog pause and lift his head, his nose and tail twitching with excitement.

Mark took a cautious step forward and cocked his rifle as quietly as he could. At the faint click a gray-brown shape moved in the swamp, fifty yards away. Through the trees he saw a ten-point buck standing alert, its big ears up and listening. The boy held his breath. Very slowly he raised the Winchester and took aim, his heart pounding as he squeezed the trigger.

The crack of the rifle was loud in the woods. The buck leaped convulsively and fell, and the two does dashed away, their white tail flags vanishing in the brush. Tige let loose with a frenzy of pent-up barking.

"Did you get him?" Buck called. "They were out o' sight from me."

"Right!" Mark answered exultantly. "An' he's a big one, too. It'll be a job to carry him out."

He ran forward to the fallen deer. His shot had reached

the heart, and the great brown eyes were already glazing when the hunter reached its side.

"Pure luck!" said Buck, pretending to be envious. "But he sure is a beauty. Look at that rack o' horns! You ought to get a head like that mounted."

"Maybe," Mark replied gruffly. The exhilaration of a good shot was all gone, and he was feeling the regret that always came when he killed an innocent wild thing.

"Come on," he said at last. "I'll take the first carry if you'll help load him across my shoulder."

The buck must have weighed close to a hundred pounds —a big one for that part of the country. Bowed forward under his burden, Mark slogged out to firmer ground and went toiling up the slope till he reached the top. There he was glad to let his friend take over.

"Too bad there isn't more snow," said Buck. "We could take him down in a hurry if we were on skis. Have you got a place to hang him at your house?"

"Sure have. Want to start over that way an' go down through the cutover land?"

Buck shook his head. "Too far," he said. "I'll run him up to your place in the pickup truck."

Turn and turnabout, they carried the limp body of the deer down the steep trail. At last they reached the Evanses' farmyard, where Buck backed the Ford pickup out of the shed. They loaded the carcass aboard and drove out to the highway.

"Bushes are looking good," Mark commented. His eyes were on the level fifteen-acre blueberry patch to their left. Long rows of the carefully cultivated bushes glowed reddish brown in the morning sun.

"All of 'em seem to be doing well," Buck answered. "I'm anxious to see how those latest Jerseys stand the winter. They ought to be all right if the ground doesn't freeze too hard before we get snow. A good thick blanket'll protect 'em an' give 'em the moisture they need. Did you hear about the new quick-freezing plant down in the village? They're starting to build it at last. Be ready to operate by the time the first berries come in, I reckon."

They were just about to turn into the dirt road at the Wilkinses' place when a car came up beside them. The driver wore a felt hat with a broad, flat brim like those of the state troopers, but he wasn't in uniform. He motioned Buck over to the ditch, then pulled up in front of the truck.

"Game warden," he announced curtly, coming to the cab door. "Pretty nice buck you have there. Let me see your hunting licenses."

He took both cards and read them carefully, then grinned. "Hi, Buck," he said. "Hi, Mark. You used to be called Buddy, didn't you? Never knew what your first names were till now. Bertram Evans, eh? An' Mark Twain Wilkins! Where'd you get a monicker like that, Mark?"

The boy squirmed. "That was my dad's idea, Mr. Jones," he said. "Named us all for writers—except Elmer. He's just a junior. Bess is Elizabeth Browning, an' Bill's William Shakespeare. Then there's Emily Dickinson an' Jane Austen. You see we're a real literary family."

With a chuckle the warden handed back their licenses. "Which one got the deer?" he asked. "An' where'd you shoot him?"

"He's Mark's," said Buck. "I was just along for the walk. We found tracks up the other side o' the mountain an' trailed 'em to the swamp."

"See any other hunters up there?" the warden asked. "Or any sign of blood, as if a deer had been killed?"

"I didn't," said Mark. "Did you, Buck? Why'd you ask, Mr. Jones?"

"I heard some shots the other night. Had a hunch somebody was market hunting—using a jack light. It's been done before up here."

"That's right," Buck put in. "I remember—back in the days when Mort Tuttle was around. I guess he just about lived on illegal deer meat an' stuff he could steal. It's a good thing he got a long stretch in state's prison."

Jones nodded and started toward his car. "Don't forget, boys," he called as he waved them on. "Today's the last day, so you'd better put your rifles up till next year."

"Sounds as if he suspected us!" Mark grumbled, but his companion laughed at the idea.

"I've known Dick Jones all my life," said Buck. "He's a square man an' one o' the best wardens in Pennsylvania."

The Wilkins house was little more than a shack, built of waste lumber and roofed with corrugated iron. Mark's father had put it together with his own unskilled hands when he moved his family to the woods. Like many writers he had been a painfully shy man and poor. His neighbors on the mountain would have been glad to help him build a more substantial house if he had asked them. But he had never taken any steps to get acquainted.

Mark wasn't ashamed of the place. It was home, and he took it for granted. The four rooms were enough to keep the family warm and dry through the colder months, and in the summer they all ran wild in the woods. Some day Mark meant to do some work on the house—make it bigger and solider—perhaps even rebuild it. But there were always other things they needed more.

Mrs. Wilkins put her head out the door as they drove into the yard. "Don't tell me you got a deer already!" she exclaimed. "I thought you'd be gone all day. Who shot it?"

"Old deadeye, here." Buck laughed. "I guess he wanted to show me up—me and my new rifle."

"My! That's a big one, isn't it?" she commented. "After it's hung a while, we'll send you some o' the meat, Buck. How are your folks?"

"Mother's fine," he replied. "Dad's about as usual, but he

doesn't do any complaining. Where's Bess? Is she around?"

As if in answer, a slim girl in her early twenties ducked under Mrs. Wilkins' arm and came running out. Shining brown hair framed her face softly, and her big eyes were alight at the sight of Buck.

"Huh!" Mark snorted. "Guess I won't get any help now hanging this deer."

He left Buck talking to his sister and drove the pickup over to the side of the yard. From the barn he brought a length of rope. In a few minutes he had flipped it over the limb of an oak tree, made one end fast to the deer's hind legs above the hocks, and hauled the carcass up till the antlers hung clear of the ground. Then he gutted it with his hunting knife and pulled the body still higher. No marauding bobcat was going to get at his venison if he could help it. Next he carefully cleaned and oiled his rifle and set it back on the pegs in the kitchen. Buck and Bess had wandered off somewhere.

"Mom," he said, "what about those two lovebirds? Think they'll ever get married?"

His mother smiled as she went on kneading dough at the breadboard. "Don't be impatient, Mark," she answered. "I know he's asked her, and I know Bess has said yes. But she wants to keep on teaching through this school year. I can't quarrel with that—goodness knows, we need the money. But as soon as you're ready to work steady, I hope they won't have to put it off any longer."

The words sobered Mark. Much as he loved his older sister, he hadn't quite realized the sacrifice she was making for her family. Now he felt the weight of a new responsibility. He was only a junior in high school. Maybe he ought not to try to finish but start thinking about a full-time job.

Outside, the brightness of the morning had turned to a dull gray, and there was a bite in the north wind. The storm he had anticipated earlier was drawing near. He saw Buck and Bess hurrying back to the house.

"Reckon you'll get that snow blanket you wanted for the berry bushes," Mark called to his friend. "There come the first flakes now."

Buck nodded. "I'm heading for home before it gets a good start," he said. He gave Bess a quick kiss, jumped into the truck, and went chugging off down the rutted road with a wave to them both.

Out of the woods the rest of the Wilkins clan came running. Elmer and Emily led the way, with little Bill and Janie close at their heels. Elmer stopped to admire the deer.

"Startin' to snow," he panted. "Think it'll be a big 'un?"

"Could be," Mark replied, looking into the thickening cloud of flakes. "You kids had better get plenty o' firewood in before you take off your things."

Chapter 2

The radio newscast at noon told of heavy snow to the west and north and warned that driving was already dangerous on the Pocono roads. The storm had settled down to business. Steadily it kept on all afternoon, and when Mark went out to the barn in the early dark to do his chores, he found himself wading through seven or eight inches of snow.

That night he got down his skis and ski poles from the chilly storage space over the rafters. The skis were a well-worn pair but a good make, and he was happy to see they had neither warped nor split. The bindings, too, were in fairly good condition. In one place mice had started to gnaw at the tough leather but had done little damage.

He warmed a can of ski wax on the back of the stove and applied it to the running surfaces, rubbing it deep into the grain of the wood. While his mother knitted, Bess was reading aloud to the younger children. It was warm and pleasant there in the kitchen, all the cozier because of the rustle of snow and the moaning wind outside.

By ten o'clock the others had gone to bed and Mark sat alone, waiting for the radio news. As far as he was concerned, it was good. The storm was expected to end by daylight Sunday with a foot or more of snow on the ground. Drifting had not been bad. The plows were out, and highways should be fairly well cleared before noon. Mark gave his skis a pat of anticipation and undressed in the chilly room he shared with the smaller boys. Soon he was asleep, dreaming of speed on the white slopes of Blueberry Mountain.

The snow had stopped falling when he woke. He put in fifteen minutes of hard work, shoveling paths to the woodpile, the barn, and the henhouse. Then he did the milking, fed the animals, and returned in time for breakfast with the other children. Elmer had a pair of hickory skis he had laboriously carved out for himself with a drawshave, and Bill had inherited the two barrel staves on which his brothers had learned. Both youngsters were as eager to get out in the snow as Mark.

As soon as breakfast was over, he pulled ski boots on over two pairs of wool socks, tied the bottoms of his trousers with string, and donned a windproof jacket and knitted ear protectors. Elmer and Bill were already on the pasture hill behind the barn. Mark left them there and started climbing on a trail through the woods. Cross-country skiing was something he enjoyed—the uphill work, tacking and herringboning, then the easy glide along level ground and the quick, smooth rush when the trail dipped downward. There in the woods it took skill to avoid the trees and make the sharp turns without breaking stride.

He had been on skis every winter since he was six, and though the only instruction he had ever had was what Buck Evans could give him, he had taught himself tricks that even a professional would have approved. Later, when he learned from books the names of such maneuvers as Christianias and Telemarks, stem swings and jump turns, he was surprised to find he had been doing them instinctively all his life.

After half an hour he broke out of the brush into more

open country, high on the slope of the mountain. This was the cutover land. It had been logged off several years before, and now, under its deep blanket of snow, it stretched invitingly down and down, all the way to the distant highway. The stumps and ledges were well covered. The only obstacles were the little pines and hemlocks that had started to grow after the logging was done.

Standing there resting on his poles, Mark sadly recalled the day when that barren slope had become the property of the Wilkins family. Buying it was one of the last things his father did. Ever since the boy could remember, they had been poor—"poor as church mice," in the words of their neighbors. Elmer Wilkins had been a writer. When things got really bad, he dashed off a short story and sent it to his literary agent. Sometimes a magazine would buy it, and the family would have groceries for a few months. But most of the time he worked on the novel that he believed would make him famous and resented any interruption.

Mrs. Wilkins respected his ambition. She taught the children to be quiet when their father was writing. Mark had sometimes peeped into the little room where he worked. Great piles of handwritten manuscript lay about, and there was a rickety typewriter his father used when he was turning out a short story.

Finally, after nearly ten years, the first draft of the book was finished. With eyes aglow and a voice that shook with emotion, Elmer Wilkins announced the fact at supper one night. Laboriously he typed the first few chapters, and a synopsis of the rest of the novel, and mailed them to his agent in New York. To the family's astonishment a publisher accepted it!

A month went by and then, out of the blue, arrived a check for two thousand dollars in advance royalties. It was more money than they had ever seen at one time. Eagerly they discussed what should be done with it.

"We can fix up the house," Bess suggested. "Put on a new roof and get some pretty curtains for the windows."

"That would be nice," her mother agreed. "We need some decent furniture, too. But first there are bills to be paid."

Mr. Wilkins had merely smiled. "I've got my own plans," he told them. "Right now I'm going to put this in the bank."

He was away most of the day. When he came home, they could see he was excited about something. At the supper table he laughed and joked and dropped hints about some wonderful news. It wasn't until they had finished eating that he told them. His thin, slouched body straightened up and a look of triumph was on his face.

"I guess," he said, "I haven't been a very good father. All your lives you children have been poor, and I know you've thought I wasn't much of a businessman. Well, today I made an investment that will change all that. I bought something that nobody can take away from us—land! And I got a lot of it. Four hundred beautiful acres at only four dollars an acre!"

They all sat speechless with amazement. It was Mark who finally broke the silence.

"Where is it?" he asked. "Where's the farm, Dad?"

His father waved an arm grandly. "Right there on the side of the mountain," he replied. "It's that whole big tract where they logged off the timber!"

The next day he had gone out in the cold March rain and spent hours proudly inspecting his new property. Soaked to the skin, he returned at nightfall, shaking with a chill. They got him to bed and called a doctor, but by that time little could be done. Within twenty-four hours he died of pneumonia.

* * *

Mark shook himself now, planted the ski poles firmly, took a couple of quick skating steps, and plunged down the slope. Faster and faster he went, the wind whistling past his ears. Dodging and twisting, he avoided the small trees and headed straight for the ledge that formed a drop-off. He knew the place well. A few yards above it he crouched, skis together. Then at the very edge he straightened his legs springily and went soaring into space. It was a glorious feeling, even though the jump was only thirty or forty feet. He landed lightly on the smooth snow below, his right ski forward and left knee bent, and the rush of speed carried him on down the more gradual slope till he brought up twenty yards from the highway. He had traveled more than half a mile in something less than a minute.

At least, he thought grimly, his father's foolish purchase had given him and his brothers a fine winter playground.

The sound of a horn made him turn toward the road. Two station wagons had pulled up there, and he saw skis nested in the racks on their tops. Each of them held four or five young people dressed in winter sports togs. Mark moved over to the side of the nearest car.

"Skiing looks pretty good up there," said a boy about his own age. "Open to the public, is it?"

" 'Fraid not," Mark replied with a laugh. "It's never been cleared right, and you'd be likely to bust a leg on the stumps an' rocks unless you knew every inch o' the hill."

"You must know it pretty well," one of the girls put in. "It looked so easy when you came down."

"I've skied it quite a few times before," he told her. "My family owns the hill. Even so, I was taking some chances."

A fat, pasty-faced youth in the rear seat was looking at the slope with scorn. "Wouldn't be much fun here, anyhow," he remarked. "There's no lift to get you to the top an' no place to buy eats an' stuff."

The rest of them laughed. "That's you, all right, Tubby," said the driver. "Might do you good to climb a hill or two. How far is it to the nearest regular ski slope, Bud?"

Mark saw the speaker was addressing him. "About fifteen miles," he answered. "It's a place called Baird's Notch. You go back to the village an' turn left. Then stay right on the highway. They've got a lodge there and a new lift, just opened. I hope you'll come back some time. Maybe I'll have this place fixed up so you can ski on it."

They waved cheerfully and turned the cars down the hill. For a moment he stood there, wondering why he had made that remark about coming back. It was the first time the idea of clearing the slope had ever entered his head.

The Evanses' place was hidden by the woods, but it was only a few hundred yards from where he stood. Now he saw Buck come out onto the highway in his car and drive toward him. The car pulled to the shoulder of the road.

"Hi!" Buck greeted him. "I'm on my way to pick up your family an' take 'em to church. Looks like you plan to play hooky this morning."

Mark nodded. "Snow's too good to miss. You'd better come out an' try it when you get back."

As soon as his friend had driven on, he climbed the hill again, keeping to one side of the cutover slope and studying the position of the rocks and stumps and young evergreens. Seen from below, they were easier to spot, for frequently the downhill sides were bare of snow. There were a lot of them. Any stranger trying to ski that slope would almost certainly be in trouble.

Mark went higher this time, climbing clear to the upper end of the logged-off tract. Cars that passed on the highway looked like tiny beetles from that distance. They were nearly a mile away, he judged, and the actual drop must be close to eight hundred feet. He took a deep breath of the clear cold air and started his descent.

Cutting to the right in a long dog-leg, he picked up the tracks of his first run and followed them down the same twisting course. Where his skis had packed it, the snow was even faster now. Again he took the jump, made a clean landing, and flashed on till he reached the level, stopping short in a swirl of snow.

There was time for one more climb and another downhill run before the car got back from church. Mark wasn't tired. He felt as if he could keep it up all day for the sake of those few moments of exhilarating speed.

Buck brought home his mother and the female members of the Wilkins family and made a quick change into his ski clothes. Soon his car appeared again and he got out, pausing only to buckle the binders on his boots.

"Kind o' rough, isn't it?" he asked Mark, looking up at the slope. "I guess I'd better follow your tracks."

"That's the safest way," Mark replied. "But there's really plenty o' snow. Come on—let's go."

Buck was a good skier, and the farm work had kept his muscles hard. Nevertheless, he was panting by the time they had climbed the first half mile.

"You must be part goat!" he told Mark. "I'm not used to this. Gimme a chance to catch my breath."

They rested a moment, then went on at an easier pace. "Say," Buck remarked, "you remember what the game warden was talking about yesterday—somebody killing deer with lights? Well, I was wrong about Mort Tuttle being safe out o' the way. After church I heard Jake Bonham say Tuttle got his parole from prison a month ago. Nobody 'round here has seen him, but that doesn't prove much. He's more at home in these woods than a fox."

Mark heard the news with a frown. "He could be the one, all right," he said. "Only if he's out on parole, he has to report, doesn't he? The state troopers must have kept track of him."

"That's what I thought, too, but Bonham claims he just dropped out o' sight. I guess we'll all have to keep an eye on our chicken houses an' lock up our doors at night."

They reached the top, adjusted the wrist straps on their poles, and prepared to take off. Mark led the way with his friend swooping close behind. Once more the younger boy took the jump at the ledge, landed, and swung into a quick turn. Buck, coming fast, was crouched for the spring. As he snapped erect at the take-off, one of his ski binders let go, and the ski spun away to the right. He tried desperately to make a landing on one foot, missed his balance, and went cartwheeling into the snow.

Worried, Mark rushed to his side. But his fears were soon set at rest. Buck sat up, roaring with laughter.

"That must have been pretty to watch!" he gasped. "Lucky I didn't break my neck. Where's that doggone ski?"

Mark went and got it. "Look at this," he said when he came back. "The strap was gnawed nearly through. Where'd you have 'em stored?"

"Up in the attic. Ma told me she thought there were squirrels up there, but I was in too much of a hurry to notice when I came out."

"All it needs is a new strap," said Mark. "I'll go down to your house with you while you fix it. Got a half-baked idea I'd like to talk over with you."

Chapter 3

They climbed into the car, and Buck backed it around. "So," he said with a chuckle, "an idea is rattling around in what you call your head. Go ahead—shoot."

Mark hesitated, trying to find the right words. "I guess," he began, "it's about making a white elephant pay for itself."

"White elephant?" questioned Buck. "You mean the cutover land?"

"Yep. A couple of carloads of skiers stopped there this morning. Said they wanted to try the slope. O' course, I told 'em no—it wasn't safe unless they knew where all the rocks an' stumps were. But after they'd gone, I got to thinking. More an' more people are going in for skiing these days. You take the kids in Crow Ridge High School. I bet half of 'em have asked for skis for Christmas. There are a few little slopes—pastures an' so on—where they can learn, but for really decent skiing they have to go all the way to Baird's Notch or farther, an' when they get there, it's expensive."

"O.K.," Buck interrupted. "I see what you're getting at. You'd like to clear that cutover slope so it would be safe. I think it's a first-class idea. Only trouble is, it would sure be a lot o' work."

"Maybe not as much as you think," said Mark. "All I'd need is a good clear lane, maybe a couple o' hundred feet wide. I figure that might be fifty or sixty stumps an' boulders to take out in the first half-mile. If I could get that much done next summer, I'd have a start on it, anyhow. And I wouldn't have to charge very much to use the slope—just enough to pay taxes."

Buck nodded. "Pulling stumps wouldn't be too tough with that little Cat tractor o' mine," he replied thoughtfully. "We could use the winch on the rear end. But I'm counting on you for full-time work as soon as school's out in the spring."

"Sure," said Mark. "But I could put in a couple of hours every evening, and I'd want you to take whatever the use o' the tractor costs out o' my wages."

Buck laughed. "Let's not worry about that," he said. "By June you'll be my brother-in-law—unless Bess postpones it again. So fixing up the slope is all in the family. Think you could make any money out of it?"

"Well, I wouldn't expect to get rich. I figure quite a few folks would be glad to pay fifty cents or a dollar to ski here. An' I thought I'd rig up some sort of a snack bar at the bottom, where we could sell things like coffee or soft drinks an' doughnuts."

"You know," said Buck, "the more you talk about it, the better it sounds. No need to start out too big. That could come later if you make a go of it on a small scale. In fact, I bet you can borrow money at the bank for expansion when the time comes. My old partner in the blueberry business works at the Crow Ridge Bank now, and he'd put in a word for you, same as I would."

"You mean Joe Sullivan? Sure—he was always a good friend o' mine. I hear he's doing all right, too."

Buck chuckled. "He's in line for the cashier's job," he replied. "Joe's always had a good head for figures, and being lame doesn't bother him, working in the bank."

They repaired the binder strap and went back to the

hill for one more run before dinnertime. As they climbed, Buck asked Mark about the prospects of the high-school basketball team.

"I hear you've got a winner this year," he said.

"Too soon to tell yet," Mark told him. "But it's a good, scrappy outfit. We won our first game easy enough. Next Friday we play Stroudsburg on their court, an' that'll be different. You'd better bring Bess an' come down there to watch us."

Buck welcomed the idea and promised to be on hand. After the downhill run they parted at the foot of the slope. Mark watched the car out of sight, then turned for a last look at the ski trails on the mountainside. In imagination he could already see it cleared of obstructions and swarming with happy skiers. It was strange how a few hours had changed his attitude toward the valueless piece of land.

* * *

Out on the gym floor, that last week before the Christmas holidays, Coach Winton worked his Crow Ridge squad hard. It wasn't a very big squad, either in stature or numbers. To get ten boys on the floor at once, he had to use a couple of freshmen. And the tallest player on the team was Moose Martin, the center, who stood six-three. Nevertheless, Winton wasn't discouraged. The youngsters had spirit, and he liked the way they kept trying.

"Come on, Wilkins," he called. "Let's see that number four weave play again. Take it from the back line."

Mark bounced the ball in to his backcourt partner, Chuck Wagner. As they passed it to and fro, he held up four fingers, then dribbled down court while the other players started their crisscross pattern. Valiantly the second team tried to set up a man-to-man defense, but the ball moved too fast from hand to hand. At the right moment Moose Martin drifted into the slot, took a high pass from Mark, and flipped it one-handed through the hoop.

"O.K., gang," said the coach. "Take a few shots from the foul line and we'll call it a day."

He talked to Mark afterward. "Stroudsburg's defense will be tougher to handle," he said, "so don't try that one too often. Drive in when you can. And if they get to expecting it, screen for Joe Rossi or Link Freeman outside. Or take a shot yourself. You can usually hit 'em from twenty feet out."

All week long they practiced, sharpening their shooting eyes. Mark was floor captain, and on him most of the plays would depend. Size wasn't necessary for a job like that. He was only five-feet-ten, but his wiry body was well coordinated. Quick and sure-footed, he could go down like lightning on a fast break, and his ball handling was well above average for a teen-ager. More than that, he kept cool under fire.

Friday came at last. As soon as classes were out, the squad got into a big yellow school bus, along with the cheerleaders and a fifteen-piece band. It was twenty miles down to Stroudsburg, and they were there by five o'clock. The coach took his players to a diner, where they ate a light, plain meal. Then they went over to the high-school gymnasium, rested a while, and got into their uniforms. For an hour they practiced, shooting fouls and becoming used to the strange floor. There was time for another rest before the game started at eight.

Quite a crowd of Crow Ridge rooters had followed the team down. It was a comfort to see their familiar faces in the stands and hear home-town cheers. As he ran out for practice under the basket, Mark caught a glimpse of his sister and Buck, three rows up, behind the bench.

All of them had pregame jitters during the warm-up, but Mark did his best to steady the rest of the squad. When the whistle blew and he was shaking hands with the man he was to guard, he felt cool and ready. Stroudsburg's lanky center outreached Moose on the jump and the game was on.

The enemy got three baskets before the Crow Ridge forwards could find the range. Then a personal was slapped on Joe Rossi. It looked to Mark as if he had merely blocked the ball, but he was called for hacking. All of a sudden the score was 7 to 0.

They brought the ball down-floor, and Mark held up four fingers. The weave was tricky, but it might help his team get back some confidence. They crisscrossed and passed for several seconds. Then a fast-moving Stroudsburg forward darted out and stole the ball from Chuck Wagner's hands. With Mark right beside him, the forward raced for the basket.

Feet were pounding behind them, and with two or three on one it looked like another sure score. Timing his stride with the dribble, Mark shot out his arm and intercepted the ball on the rise. Then, before the pursuers could change direction, he threw a long baseball pass back to Moose Martin, all alone under the basket. With plenty of time, the big center dropped it through, and at last Crow Ridge fans had something to cheer about.

After that the boys from up the mountain settled down. They stayed with their opponents on defense, grabbed their share of rebounds, and began hitting with their shots. At half time they were trailing by only three points—30 to 27.

They didn't go back to the dressing room, for the Stroudsburgers were there. Chip Winton gathered his group around him on the bench and talked to them while he massaged a pulled muscle in Link Freeman's leg.

"I'd like to see some fast breaking this half," he said. "Moose, keep getting those rebounds. And the second you do, pass down-floor. I think we can outrun some of those big guys. Link, I'm going to keep you out till toward the end. We may need you then, so wrap that leg up warm and get some rest. Sam Bonham'll go in for you, to start off."

They limbered up under the basket and took their places once more for the jump. Mark felt strong and ready to go. On the tap, Moose deflected the ball toward him, and he dribbled past the man guarding him, faked a pass, and took a long jump shot that banked off the board and went in. A dozen seconds later, Stroudsburg retaliated with a score. Then Joe Rossi was fouled in the act of shooting. The goal counted, and he arched in his foul shot perfectly to bring them even at 32-all.

The tie didn't last long. Stroudsburg's tall pivot man dunked an easy lay-up. Then, as Crow Ridge brought it down, a pass to Sam Bonham went through his fingers and right into the hands of an opposing guard. There was a quick race down the floor, a flurry of arms under the basket, and a lucky shot that went in. Once more Stroudsburg had a four-point lead.

Try as they would, Crow Ridge couldn't seem to narrow the gap. With three minutes left to play, they still trailed by 47-43. At that point Stroudsburg called a time out. To Mark's dismay he saw four new men come off the bench, all as big as the starters they replaced.

"Don't let that worry you," Coach Winton told his team. "All it means is that their first-string boys are tired. These new ones may be fresher, but they won't be as good shots and ball handlers. How's the leg feel, Link? O.K., go on in. Let's show 'em, gang!"

Stroudsburg had the ball for the throw-in. Mark watched two lazy passes go by, then suddenly jumped high to intercept the ball in the air. Dribbling like a fiend, he was under the basket a half stride ahead of the pursuit and made his lay-up shot. In spite of Crow Ridge's all-court press, their opponents managed to get the ball across the mid-line. After a lot of weaving and passing, one of them tried a twenty-foot set shot. It hit the backboard and bounced out into Moose Martin's waiting hands. Mark had guessed it might happen and was already sprinting down the floor. He turned just as the center's long heave came toward him, caught it, and passed across to Link, a dozen feet from the basket. The forward's one-hand jump shot arched through without even touching the rim.

With the score 47-all, the Stroudsburg coach hastily sent his varsity players back in. The clock showed only two minutes remaining. On the next play Moose tried to block a shot by the opposing center and had a foul called on him. The lanky player missed his first shot from the foul line, but his second went in. Then it was Stroudsburg's turn to put on a press and try to get possession of the ball.

Mark brought it down cautiously, dribbling just out of reach of his overeager opponent. There was no hurry. He wanted the next shot to be good, and he signaled for the weave. Handling their passes neatly, his mates kept the circle gradually narrowing. Then the ball came to Mark. Like lightning he drove in, but with flailing arms all around him a shot was impossible. He made a quick bounce pass out to Joe Rossi. The forward took it on the rise and flipped a beautiful one-hander through the hoop. The scoreboard showed Crow Ridge ahead by 49-48, with less than a minute left to play.

Chip Winton called a time out now. "Boys," he told his panting players, "they'll be trying to get the last shot. But they won't dare stall around too long. If they shoot and miss, we've got to get the rebound. If they score, don't let it bother you. We'll still have time to make the last basket. Whatever you do, don't foul!"

Stroudsburg brought the ball in and met little resistance as they came down the court. The seconds were ticking away. But as the coach had foreseen, the pressure of time was too much for a keyed-up high-school team that trailed

by a point. With fifteen seconds to go, a nervous backcourt man let fly with a set shot. It skimmed around the rim and fell off, with Moose Martin leaping high to grab it. He twisted away and threw another long pass down to Mark.

The mountain boy wasn't alone this time. A husky Stroudsburg forward raced with him toward the basket. Mark checked his stride, looked around as if to pass, then jumped with a one-hander. At the last split second his opponent tried desperately to block the shot and hacked his arm. But the ball was on its way. It hesitated on the rim and fell through while the Crow Ridge rooters screamed their delight.

Calmly Mark went to the foul line to complete his three-point play. He drew a long, steadying breath, fixed his eyes on the basket, and swished the ball in. Before Stroudsburg could get off another shot, the clock ran out. Crow Ridge had beaten its strongest rival by a 52-48 score.

Chapter 4

It was snowing when the squad went out to the bus for the trip home. There was little wind, and the flakes floated down, big and soft.

"On top o' what we've got already," Mark told Moose Martin, "this ought to make some pretty good skiing. Have you done any yet?"

"No," said Moose, "but I'd like to. How 'bout tomorrow? I could take a bunch of us in my folks' station wagon an' head over to Baird's Notch."

Mark hesitated. It cost money to ski there, but he really ought to take a look at the layout.

"O.K.," he said. "I'll be ready by eight if you can pick me up. I've got a job at Beaver Lake for the holidays, but it doesn't start till Monday. See you tomorrow, then."

It was about ten-thirty when the team bus reached Crow Ridge that night, and Buck's car was waiting there when Mark got off. Bess waved at him from the right-hand window.

"Come on, hero!" she called. "We'll take you home."

He climbed in beside her, and they drove off up the mountain. Buck was full of the game.

"Nice job, kid," he said. "Do you know how many points you scored?"

"No," replied Mark truthfully. "I didn't keep track. Nine or ten, I guess."

"Well, I'll tell you—you were top scorer. Six field goals an' three fouls—fifteen points."

"That right?" Mark asked. "All I knew was we pulled out a win."

Bess laughed and squeezed his arm. "That's my modest little brother!" she said. "Anyway, we're proud of you, Mark!"

She heated some cocoa when they got home, and the three of them sat in the kitchen for a while, talking in low voices so as not to wake the sleeping family.

"I told Bess about your idea," said Buck. "Fixing up a ski slope, I mean. I reckon she likes it."

"Of course I do," Bess replied. "I'm tired of hearing people run down Dad's business judgment. This looks like a practical way to put the property to work."

"Put *me* to work, you mean." Mark laughed. "I'll have to do some sweating before we'd want to let strangers ski on it. That reminds me—I'd better get to bed. Tomorrow a bunch of us are going to Baird's Notch an' see what they've done over there."

He was up at dawn and raced through the morning chores. A little after eight he took his skis and poles and went down to the highway, where the Martin station wagon soon appeared. Four other boys were inside, and their skis were racked on top.

The gang was in a hilarious mood. "Look at that snow!" cried Chuck Wagner. "Four or five inches o' new powder on a good base! We ought to get some good fast runs today."

"All you guys think about," said Mark, "is schussing downhill. If you'd come up an' run some cross-country trails with me, you'd learn what real skiing is like."

Chuck laughed. "That's for the birds," he answered. "Me—I want a nice, comfortable chair to take me up the hill."

But Moose agreed with Mark. "That's why you'll never be a top-notch skier," he told Chuck. "Riding chairs doesn't develop any muscles or teach you how to handle yourself on a fast slope."

It was before nine when they reached the ski lodge at Baird's Notch. But the hillside was already lined with tracks, and the lift was in operation. Fifty or sixty cars stood in the parking area, with more arriving every minute.

A number of low, rustic buildings were clustered at the foot of the slope. The lodge itself had two stories, with rooms and dormitories upstairs. On the ground floor a cheerful log fire blazed on the wide hearth, and the room was bright with colorful ski costumes. Men and girls swarmed around the long lunch counter, and the cashier's desk was doing a brisk business.

They got in line to buy their tickets—two dollars for a day on the slope, and twenty-five cents for each ride to the top. Mark looked at the prices with dismay. He had less than four dollars in his pocket. One trip on the lift was all he felt he could afford.

Outside in the bracing air they put on their skis. "Think I'll climb, this first time," Mark told the others. "I'd like to get the feel o' the snow an' study the run a bit. Anybody want to come along?"

Moose was the only one willing to go up on skis. As they toiled upward, one after another of their friends went swooping past down the trail. Chuck Wagner waved gaily, then hit a small bump and lost his balance, sitting down hard. They helped him up but didn't laugh at him. The tumble, while not painful, had already deflated his opinion of himself as a skier.

"Come on," said Moose. "Climb back up with us. You'll get a better idea what the slope's like an' where the trouble spots are."

But Chuck's injured dignity wouldn't permit it. He said he preferred to schuss the rest of the hill and go up again on the lift.

There were three main trails on the slope, all starting close together at the top. They followed different gradients down the hillside but converged once more at the foot. One was called the "Kitten"—descending in long, gentle curves and nowhere very steep. Over on the opposite side was a trail known as the "Tail-Wagger." It made half a dozen sharp switchbacks as it twisted through the woods, with plenty of opportunity for Christies and swing turns. The middle trail, dropping down the three-quarter-mile slope with hardly a curve, was the "Fool-Killer." It had the straightaway speed that the more daring skiers liked. Some of them came to grief. Even as the boys watched, they saw the ski patrol hauling away a reckless youngster who appeared to have twisted his leg.

"A guy's crazy to take that kind of a hill before he really knows what he's doing," Mark growled. "That's why Americans don't score better in the tough competitions like the Winter Olympics. Want to run before they can walk."

Moose Martin agreed. "I guess if you grow up on skis, like the Scandinavians," he said, "you learn how to handle any kind o' going. A fellow I know who's been over there says kids in Norway ski a dozen miles to school over the mountains, an' do it every day. No wonder they beat us in cross-country races—an' downhill, too."

They reached the top, where skiers were dropping off the lift chairs in a steady stream. Mark did some mental arithmetic as he watched them. The proprietors of the slope must have taken in five hundred dollars already, he figured, and the day was still young. Of course, they couldn't count on many weekends like this, but there was no question they were making money.

"Which one you want to try?" asked Moose.

"I sort o' like that twisty one—the 'Tail-Wagger,'" Mark replied. "It's got some stiff turns, but the snow's still pretty fresh. Not too many folks have been down that way, I guess."

A girl, skiing alone, took off just ahead of them. She was graceful and fast. The way she handled her sticks and edged her skis on the first turn showed she had had experience. Mark felt the cold air streaming past his face as he swooped after her.

The trail followed the fall line of the mountain, back and forth, dropping just enough for plenty of speed. There were trees on both sides, and some of the curves had to be made sharply to avoid them. Mark stemmed without losing pace, sped down a short incline toward the woods, and swung hard to the right in a single-pole jump turn. The next curve was to the left, and he took it with a Christie, his legs and arms moving in perfect balance.

The girl, he thought, must be just around the next bend, for he had been coming down fast. But the slope was empty below him when he made the turn. Then he caught a glimpse of her red parka. She was floundering in the snow at the edge of the woods, a hundred yards down the hill.

Quickly Mark cut across to her, plowing to a stop in a swirl of snow. "Hi, there," he said. "Are you hurt?"

She turned a woebegone face up to him and tried to smile. "Not—not really," she answered. "I must have taken the turn too wide and hit a root or something."

He took her mittened hand and helped her up, glad to see that she could stand. Sure enough, an ugly-looking root jutted out of the snow where she had fallen. The toe of one ski must have caught on it as she rounded the turn.

"That thing ought to be cut out," he told her. "It's dangerous. We'd better report it at the lodge."

She threw back the hood of her parka, and something

about her brown curls and the sparkle of her blue eyes seemed familiar to him. But for the moment he couldn't imagine where he had seen her.

"Thanks," she said with a smile. "I was bound I'd beat you down—and I bet I'd have made it, too, if I hadn't been careless. My name's Jean Langley. What's yours?"

"Mark Wilkins," he replied. "Though a few people still call me Buddy. Say—I wonder—do you stay at Beaver Lake in the summer?"

"Why, yes," she said with a laugh. "We're from Philadelphia, but this weekend we opened up our cottage. Do you know Beaver Lake?"

"Sure do. I live four or five miles from there, on Blueberry Mountain. You wouldn't remember, but I used to deliver berries at the Langleys' cottage. I thought I'd seen you before."

Moose Martin arrived just then and was introduced. "You folks are too fast for me," he told them with a grin.

"Those turns are so sharp, I was doing snowplows to get around."

The girl checked her skis and binders and slapped some of the snow from her clothes. "Well," she said, "I'll have a few black and blue spots tomorrow, but right now let's finish this run."

They followed her down, admiring her skill and the plucky way she swept into the turns. Apparently the tumble had done nothing to daunt her courage. At the foot of the slope she waved to them and was immediately lost in a crowd of boys and girls who seemed to be her friends.

Mark and Moose went over to the chair lift, where one or two of their own gang were waiting to go up. It was a handsome affair, mounted on steel towers, with the chairs suspended from constantly moving cables. A big electric motor, housed in a brick shed at the foot, supplied the power.

"What do you reckon a rig like this would cost?" Mark asked his big friend.

"Plenty," said Moose. "I heard this one came to more'n thirty thousand dollars. Up in Vermont an' the Adirondacks, they've got some that cost a heap more'n that."

"Gee!" Mark breathed. "No wonder they charge to ride on 'em. Well, I guess it's up to us to help 'em pay for it."

He swung aboard the next chair that came by and was soon swaying upward, high above the slope. To one side he could see little figures flashing down the "Fool-Killer." And over beyond the woods two or three skiers were taking the twisting turns of the trail he had run.

In what seemed no time at all, he was at the top. Moose stood beside him, looking down the steep middle hill. "Let's go," he told Mark with a grin. "Can't break our necks but once."

They waited till the slope was fairly clear, then took off. The first drop almost took their breath away. Below was a gentler grade, a bump, then another fast schuss. At its foot came a sort of dog-leg to the right. The turn wasn't sharp, but it had to be taken at high speed. Almost at once the trail bent to the left again and opened out on the straight, smooth run to the bottom. Mark skimmed down like a bird. Moose had been more cautious, but he made it a moment later without trouble.

"Whew!" gasped the big center. "I bet we were going a mile a minute on that last stretch!"

"It's fast, all right," said Mark, "but it isn't what I call real skiing. I've seen places nearer home where I can have more fun."

He was thinking of the cutover land on Blueberry Mountain. Perhaps he ought to plan on clearing two trails—one straight down and another more winding. He thought there might be room for both if he could get the necessary work done.

They climbed to the top again and took another shot at the "Tail-Wagger" before lunch. The lodge was jammed with skiers—two hundred people at least, Mark thought. But a small refreshment booth across the road had sandwiches and coffee, and it was there that they ate.

The stocky mountain woman behind the counter greeted them cheerfully. "We ain't rightly part o' the setup over there," she said, "but ye'll find the sandwiches fresher an' the prices some lower here. How's the snow? Looks good, from the number o' folks that's come out."

"It's fine," Mark told her. "Real good skiing." He looked around at the simple frame construction of the booth. "Your husband build this?" he asked.

"Yep—him an' me together. Didn't cost us but a few dollars, an' we take in quite a bit on a good weekend. Have to dress warm, though, or we'd freeze solid."

She stamped her feet and pulled a heavy shawl closer around her shoulders. "Next week," she went on, "I've told Bill we got to put in a stove o' some kind."

The sandwiches were as good as she claimed, and the coffee was strong and hot. A dozen other skiers came across the road before the boys left. It looked as if the little place would be successful.

They went back to the lodge to warm up for a few minutes before returning to the slopes. Jean Langley was sitting by the fire and beckoned to Mark to come over. She introduced him to another girl and two boys who were with her.

"We're going to be at our camp for two weeks," she said. "Why don't you come over some evening?"

He thanked her and explained that he had chores to do. "But I'll be working in the woods at Beaver Lake every day," he said. "So maybe I'll see you. I guess you'll spend most o' the time over here, though."

"Probably," she told him with a smile. "But drop in

anyway. I'd appreciate some pointers from a skier as good as you."

He flushed at the compliment and made an awkward exit. Several more times that afternoon he climbed the slope without using the lift. The last time he took a final crack at the "Fool-Killer," racing down all out. By then the Crow Ridge boys were ready to head for home.

Mark did the chores by lantern light and crawled into bed, tired but strangely happy. For one thing, he had made friends with a very pretty girl. But more important, he was certain now, in his own mind, that his idea for a ski slope would work.

Chapter 5

Sunday was still fair and cold. There had been very little melting on the side of Blueberry Mountain and the skiing had stayed good. In the afternoon Mark took young Elmer with him and climbed the cutover slope. This time he was counting the young trees that would have to be removed. The stumps and rocks were covered deep in snow, but he already knew where they were.

"Come on," his fourteen-year-old brother urged. "What are you messin' around here for? Let's go on up to the top."

"Go ahead," Mark told him. "Right now I've got business here. Some day I'll tell you all about it."

Elmer's curiosity was aroused, but he could get no more out of his brother. He clambered up the slope, and ten minutes later Mark saw him schussing down like a veteran. In spite of the clumsy home-made skis, the youngster handled himself well. He had the same fast reflexes and natural balance that made Mark a good skier.

On Monday morning the chores had to be done early. It was barely daylight when Mark set out for Beaver Lake. Instead of trying to thumb a ride on the highway, he took a woods trail southward, gliding along on his skis. Most of the four-mile trip was downhill, so he was able to make good time. Before eight o'clock he went in through the stone gateway and followed the lake-shore road to the office in the main clubhouse. Mr. Ackroyd, the superintendent, was there to greet him.

"I see you came on skis," he said. "Good idea, with this deep snow. The rest o' the crew's down there by the truck, ready to start. Dan Kelly's in charge, and he'll tell you what to do."

There were six men in the woods crew, most of them local farmers who knew Mark. Kelly himself was a big, genial Irishman who worked at the lake the year round. When they were all in the truck, they drove along a narrow trail into the forest. At the end of half a mile or so they stopped, and Kelly handed out axes and crosscut saws.

"We're goin' to clear out all the dead stuff an' thin the young trees," he said. "I'll show you the ones I want cut."

Mark was assigned to trimming off the limbs after the trees were felled, for he had done enough chopping in his life to be a good axman. There were no loafers in the crew, and the job went steadily all morning. By noon they

had thinned out a considerable area. Trunks and branches, sawed to cordwood length, were piled neatly beside the trail.

"Git aboard!" yelled Dan Kelly. "They got a hot lunch fer us back there."

The dining camp was closed for the winter, but Mrs. Ackroyd's own kitchen was roomy and warm. The men brushed snow off their boots and went in bashfully.

"Sit down, boys," the beaming woman told them, pointing to the long wooden table. "I told John you'd get more work done in the woods if you had a good hot meal under your belts. So light right in and eat your fill."

They loaded their plates with steaming beef stew, added home-baked bread and butter, and finished off with apple pie. Half an hour later they went cheerfully back to the woods, grateful to the good sense and good will of the superintendent's wife.

At five o'clock Mark got a ride home with one of the men in the crew. He was weary by the time the evening chores were done, but he liked his job. Ten dollars a day was good pay in the mountains, and he thought he could save some of it toward the work on the slope.

In the night the wind shifted to the south. Mark woke, too warm under the heavy quilts, and heard the gurgle of water running off the eaves. It was a thaw that would spoil the skiing. That morning he had to wade through the slush to the highway. After a few minutes a car appeared and gave him a ride.

Working in the dark, wet woods was less fun than it had been the day before, but there was one compensation. Some time in the afternoon a station wagon drove in along the trail. The boys and girls staying at the Langleys' camp had come to watch the operation. Mark took a minute off to say hello.

"Hi!" Jean laughed. "No skiing today, so we're just

doing some exploring. We heard the sound of the axes. Why don't you come over when you're through? I'll drive you home."

"In my work clothes?" he said. "Well, O.K.—I'd like to. But I won't be able to stay very long. Got a cow to milk."

At five o'clock he clumped up to the door of the Langleys' cottage in his worn old high-buckled rubbers. There were lights inside, and he heard the beat of a rock-and-roll dance tune played on a phonograph. Mrs. Langley came at his knock.

"Oh," she said with a smile, "you must be the Wilkins boy. Do come in and take off your things."

He had already met the young people in the house party. The two boys were obviously well-bred sons of Main Line families, both students at Penn Charter. The other girl, like Jean, went to Baldwin School in Bryn Mawr. They took him in as if he were one of them, and he was soon enjoying cider and popcorn in front of the fire.

The crowd seemed sincerely interested in what he told them in response to their many questions. It was with some pride that he described the writing his father had done.

"He was a quiet, shy kind of man," he said, "but he knew how to put words together. Next year we hope his novel will be published. My sister's working on the manuscript, typing it up, but it's a long, slow job. He left a whole stack o' paper covered with pencil writing, an' some o' the sheets got mixed up. So she has to sort it out as she goes. The publishers keep asking for the rest o' the book, so I guess they aim to bring it out, all right."

Before he knew it the clock struck six.

"Sorry," he exclaimed, jumping up. "Old Doxie's probably mooing her head off waiting to be fed an' milked."

Jean went out with him to the car. She was an excellent

driver, and they plowed through the slushy roads without trouble. As they passed the Blueberry Mountain slope, Mark pointed up at the cutover land.

"That's ours," he said. "Some day, when I get it cleared right, you'll have to come an' try the skiing."

Jean stopped the station wagon and looked at the hill. The rain had ended, and a moon lit up the white expanse.

"Why, it's a beautiful slope!" she told him. "And so handy to Beaver Lake, too! You'd be doing us a big favor if you opened it for skiers."

He was pleased. "If we get some more good snow while you're here," he said, "come over an' try it. I can show you a safe trail that dodges the stumps, an' anybody that skis the way you do could have some fun. O' course," he added, "there's no fancy lift. You'd have to go up afoot, the way I do."

"I'd love it." She laughed. "All we need now is a good storm."

She let him out at the foot of the track that led up to his home and waved good-by as she turned the car.

* * *

Mark watched the weather hopefully the next few days, but Christmas came and went with no additional snow. He kept on working at the lake, catching occasional glimpses of the Langley house-party group. Then they were gone, and the stout board shutters on the windows showed the cottage stood empty.

Finally came his last day's work before going back to school. At five o'clock Mr. Ackroyd paid him off, and he went home with a hundred dollars in crisp new tens in his pocket. He knew his mother needed the money for housekeeping expenses and tried to give it to her. However, she refused to take it all. Four of the bills, she insisted, should be his to keep.

After the milking was done, he came in to find Bess

struggling with the old typewriter. She was almost in tears.

"Only three more chapters to go," she said. "And this miserable machine has to get cranky. It seems as if I'll never finish now."

Mark didn't know much about typewriters, but he had some mechanical skill. He took the contraption apart, found where a small screw had fallen out, and dug through the screws and nails in his father's old tobacco tin till he found one that would fit. Then he touched up some of the rattling parts with gun oil and called his sister back.

"Reckon she'll hold together for the rest o' the book," he told her. "Once it's published, there ought to be some more money coming in. Enough to buy a new machine, anyhow."

"I think of that, every page I type," she said. "It's a wonderful story, though, and I enjoy working on it. Seems as if I could hear Dad's voice in some of the passages. I'm making a carbon copy, so you'll have a chance to read it when I've sent the manuscript off."

"Swell," said Mark. "What's it called?"

"Daddy never got around to giving it a title, but it's a mountain story, about this part of the country. I'd thought we might call it "Mine Eyes Unto the Hills"—you know—from the hundred-and-twenty-first psalm. If the publishers don't like that, they can name it anything they want."

The first Monday in the new year Mark was back at school. Between basketball practice and keeping up his grades, he had to work hard. But at least he was satisfied with the basketball season. They won fourteen games and lost only five, playing bigger schools nearly every week. There was no chance to get into the play-offs for the regional championship, but Coach Winton was more than satisfied.

Through January and February the skiing had been spotty. Then suddenly, on the fourth of March, it started snowing in earnest. That was a storm that old-timers could only compare to the famous "blizzard of eighty-eight." Two days of snow and wind piled the drifts ten feet deep in many places. Roads were blocked for days. Farmhouses were cut off. With the schools closed, Mark and Buck cruised the mountain area on skis, carrying food to neighbors and helping them shovel out tunnels to their barns.

When the plows were finally able to get through, the whole countryside lay under a three-foot blanket of white. Then came the skiers. The first sunny weekend after the storm they arrived in droves. And to Mark's delight, the Langleys were among them.

He was out on the Blueberry Mountain slope when he saw Jean stop her station wagon by the roadside. He whizzed down to welcome her, pleased to see that she had come alone.

She was bright-eyed and rosy in the cold. "With snow like this I just couldn't keep away," she said with a laugh. "So I persuaded Mother and Dad to come up for the weekend. How's your ski slope? It looks perfect!"

Mark helped her adjust her skis and led the way up the hill. She made the climb without difficulty. At the top they rested a few minutes while he pointed out the best route down.

"Not that you'll have any trouble today," he said. "The snow's so deep, all the stumps are covered, an' you can spot the little trees easy enough. Just follow me if you're ready."

She nodded and he took off. The trail he chose was fast but had a number of tricky curves. Once or twice he glanced back to find her right at his heels, so he cut loose with more power, taking the turns at racing speed. The final schuss to the foot of the slope had all the thrills of the Baird's Notch "Fool-Killer."

Just as he edged his skis for the stop, she shot past him,

swung into a perfect Christie, and wound up at his side, flushed and laughing.

"Golly!" he exclaimed, his voice full of respect. "Where'd you learn to ski like that?"

"I'm glad you think I'm good," Jean answered seriously. "From you that's a compliment. You see, when I was just a kid—eleven or twelve—a rich aunt took me to Europe for a year. I went to school in Switzerland, where we skied every day. Of course there were wonderful pros to teach us—Austrians and Frenchmen and Norwegians. They sort of took a fancy to the little Yankee girl and spent a lot of time on me. Believe it or not, I once won a cup in the Junior Ladies' Slalom at St. Moritz!"

"Gee!" said Mark. "Don't you go in for competition now? You'd be a real star if you kept at it."

"No," she told him, "I'm not ambitious that way. After that winter abroad, I was glad to come home and settle down to being an ordinary schoolgirl. The only skiing I do now is for fun. Come on—let's go up again. I like this slope of yours."

They made two more flying trips down the trail before noon. With some hesitancy Mark invited the girl to lunch, and she accepted.

"Don't expect to see much of a place," he told her. "It's a roof over our heads an' that's about all. But I guarantee the grub'll be good. Mom's one o' the best cooks on the mountain."

It took more than the arrival of a fashionable guest to upset Mrs. Wilkins. She welcomed Jean heartily and ordered the younger children to make room for her at the table, set in the kitchen. Bess was in Stroudsburg doing some shopping, but all the rest of the clan were introduced.

"What a grand big family!" Jean laughed. "Being an only child myself, I really envy you, Mark."

The main dish was fried collops of venison in rich

brown gravy, and the girl raved about it. When she learned that Mark had shot the buck, her eyes widened in admiration.

"You're a real woodsman, aren't you?" she said to him afterward. "I can just imagine the fun you have, up here all year long. It makes living in the suburbs seem pretty dull."

Mark chuckled. "All in the way you look at it, I reckon. Plenty o' times when I had to go out to milk in the cold at five o'clock in the morning, I've wished I was a city boy."

They skied most of the afternoon, then stopped at the Evanses' farm to say hello to Buck and look at the blueberry plantation. As dusk fell, Jean got into her car to go back to Beaver Lake.

"Thanks, Mark," she said. "It's been a day to remember. Next year, when you've cleared the slope, let's do this often!"

Chapter 6

Snow in the Poconos doesn't hang on as it does in the White Mountains or the Laurentians. By April most of the slopes lay bare. The smaller Wilkins children, home from exploring the woods, reported that skunk cabbage and jack-in-the-pulpit were up. And on the way to school Mark saw a robin in a dooryard.

He didn't go out for baseball that spring. Buck Evans needed his help in the blueberry patch, and by coming home as soon as classes were out, he could put in two or three hours of work before dark. First the ground had to be cultivated with the tractor, steering carefully down the rows between the adult bushes. Then new land was prepared to receive the small plants from the cold frames. Transplanting the young shoots was a delicate job that had to be done by hand. Afterward they hauled in swamp muck to pack around the new bushes.

The low flat ground was wet at this time of year, and a wheel tractor would have mired to the hubs. But the little Cat was fitted with extra-wide crawler tracks that didn't sink in.

By the first of May most of the early work was out of the way, and Buck suggested it was time to start pulling a few stumps on the cutover slope. Mark, of course, was delighted. He had already started Elmer trimming out the young pines and birch trees.

"Chop 'em real close to the ground," he told his younger brother, "an' carry 'em over in the woods. Be sure you do your cutting inside the stakes."

A month before, as soon as the snow melted, he had laid out a ski trail. Starting at the foot it was about a hundred yards wide, but higher up it narrowed to thirty or forty yards. With a bundle of stakes and an ax, Mark had climbed the slope, setting his boundaries. The trail had a couple of bends in it to make for more interesting skiing. It cut diagonally across the hillside, then switched back in a wide curve, and finally plunged the last quarter mile in a straight schuss.

After marking the trail, he studied the stumps and boulders that would have to be removed. Most of them looked as if they could be pulled out with the tractor, but there was one ledge of rock up near the top that would almost certainly have to be blasted. The more he looked the trail over, the surer he felt that the job could be finished before winter.

He was high on the slope one evening, clearing brush and saplings with Elmer, when Buck came up to join them. Mark pointed out the ledge to his future brother-in-law.

"Think we could get that out with dynamite?" he asked.

Buck was doubtful. "It's pretty long," he said. "Must be forty or fifty feet o' rock there. Why don't you just swing the trail east a bit, with a curve around the end o' the ledge? You'd still have enough drop so skiers wouldn't be slowed up. If we have to do any blasting, I'd say the place is lower down, where some o' those big boulders are."

Following this advice, Mark changed the position of the stakes. It lengthened the trail a little and added another turn, which he thought was all to the good. The slope would still be fast enough and a better test of skiing ability.

When Saturday came, they made an early start with the tractor. Some of the largest stumps were in the lower ground near the road, and it was these that they tackled first. With a few strokes of his ax Mark cut through the roots on the upper side. Then a chain was put around the stump and the little Cat went to work. It was surprising to see how much traction it had. Usually, after a couple of stout pulls, the whole stump came out of the ground with a rending groan. If that failed, a slower pull with the winch would do the job. By noon a dozen stumps were dragged out and piled for burning.

"How many do you figure there'll be in all?" Buck asked.

"I counted seventy-one," said Mark. "Plus maybe twenty rocks."

"Easy!" his friend replied with a grin. "We could finish in a week if we didn't have other things to do. You plan to leave that lowest ledge for a jump, don't you?"

"Sure. Anybody that doesn't want to take it can go one side or the other. It just makes the slope more sporting, far as I'm concerned."

They stood there trying to imagine the trail as it would look covered with a foot or two of snow. It made a satisfying picture.

When Mark came back after lunch, he was surprised to see seven or eight boys working with Elmer. Some had brought their own axes. Others were busy carrying away the cut brush.

His brother answered his unspoken question with a chuckle. "They're all from my class at school," he said. "When I told 'em what we were doing, they wanted to help. Every one of 'em plans to come up here an' ski next winter."

Mark moved on to the Evanses' place, for there was more work to be done in the blueberry plantation. He

and Buck were spreading muck that afternoon, hoeing it into place around the individual bushes. They moved along side by side, each in his own row.

"Got things settled with the manager of the freezer plant yesterday," Buck announced. "He'll pay twenty cents a pound for all the berries I can let him have. That doesn't sound like a lot when we get up to fifty cents a quart for home-delivered berries, but it saves the work o' sorting an' packing the boxes an' putting on the cellophane. I told him I'd have to hold back enough to take care o' my regular customers at Beaver Lake, but I figured I could still let him have twenty thousand pounds—about half the crop. He'll buy from ten or a dozen other farmers who've put in blueberries, provided they're up to our standard. An' they'll all carry our label—Pocono Sky-Blues."

"Sounds like a good deal all 'round," Mark told him. "It ought to get some more growers started if there's a steady market at that price."

"That's right," Buck agreed. "I aim to clear some more ground myself next fall. We could double the production here without overexpanding. Won't have to hire more labor, either, as long as we can count on the Wilkins family to do our picking."

Mark laughed. "No shortage o' help there," he said. "An' the kids get better at it every year. By the way, have you an' Bess set the date yet?"

"Yep," Buck replied, reddening a little. "Last Saturday in June, after school lets out. That'll give us a chance to go away for a week or two before the summer work gets heavy. Joe Sullivan's agreed to be my best man, an' I reckon it'll be up to you to give the bride away."

He saw Mark's jaw drop and gave a chuckle. "Don't worry," Buck said. "You won't have to wear a cutaway an' striped pants. Just shine up your shoes an' get a haircut."

It was after six and the sun was setting behind Blueberry

Mountain when they finished work. The highway was only a hundred yards away, and as they turned back toward the farmhouse, a jeep panel truck went scuttling past. It was gray and mud-spattered and bore no name on the side.

"Who do you s'pose that was?" asked Mark. "I couldn't get a look at the man's face through that dirty windshield. Ever see the truck before?"

"Not that I can remember," said Buck. "But quite a few folks over Bear Creek way drive jeeps. Prob'ly just a farmer on his way home."

"Funny thing about it," Mark went on thoughtfully, "was that I didn't see any license plate. Either there wasn't any or it was so covered with mud it didn't show. The guy'll be in trouble if a state cop spots him."

* * *

As the end of school approached, Mark had the strange feeling that he was living in two worlds. He studied hard for his final exams and passed with good marks, well up in the top quarter of the junior class. His mother and Bess wanted him to go to college after graduation, and it was for them that he tried to keep his grades high. At school all the seniors were excited about the final events of the year—dates for the prom—the class picnic—the chances of getting into college. And he shared some of their excitement.

Yet with the other half of his mind he thought constantly about earning money during the summer, finishing the ski slope, and building some kind of rough shelter at its foot. Somehow he had to replace the family income that Bess had provided.

Earlier he had taken the preliminary College Board examinations and thought he had done pretty well. Perhaps by this time next year he would be applying for college admission. Penn State was where he thought he'd like to go. If he was accepted, it would mean being away for most of the winter, and Elmer and the kids would have to keep the ski run operating. On the other hand, he might not get into college. He knew how disappointed his family would be, but personally he didn't care too much. After all, Buck hadn't had a college education, and he had made a success of the farm. About all he could do, Mark thought, was let fate decide. In the meantime, he had a busy summer ahead and a final year of school.

Commencement week passed in a flurry of activity. The diplomas were handed out before an admiring audience of relatives. The seniors bade each other farewell amid vows of eternal friendship. And Mark came back up the mountain to go to work.

He was looking over the blueberry plantation next morning when Buck joined him.

"Grovers an' Rubels are about done blooming," Mark said. "An' did you notice the size o' the green berries on those Pioneers down by the creek? Three or four weeks o' warm weather an' the first ones'll be ready to pick!"

Buck smiled. "Looks like an early crop, but you never can tell up here. We might get a cold spell. Anyhow, I'm not going to let it spoil my honeymoon. If we're not back by the time they ripen, you an' the kids can handle the job. Put the first ones in quart boxes an' sell 'em at the lake, the way we always have. Then, when it looks as if there'll be a steady supply, you can start delivering at the freezer plant. But I reckon we'll be here before then."

They strolled back to the higher ground, where the later-bearing varieties were planted. A soft, steady humming of bees filled the air. Three years before, Buck had started a couple of hives, and now the insects were hard at work, gathering honey and cross-pollenizing the blossoms.

There were home-grown cuttings from mountain bushes set out in alternate rows with the late varieties of Jerseys. Carefully chosen for the size of their berries, they had done well. Buck looked at them proudly.

"This whole section," he told Mark, "comes from bushes you found. Remember when I used to give you a quarter for every extra good one you located? Well, this summer I'll bet they yield as many berries—and as big ones—as the bushes we brought in from New Jersey!"

Mark laughed. "You'll be paying for some more before the summer's over," he said. "Emily an' Bill an' Janie are all planning to find bushes an' collect quarters."

Back at the barn, where the packing would be done, Buck showed Mark the trays he had bought for taking bulk berries to the freezing plant. They were of wood, six inches deep, built to hold about fifty pounds of fruit and to stack well in the pickup truck. There was also a big supply of quart boxes and many rolls of cellophane, ready to pack the berries they would sell at retail. Barring a hailstorm or some other disaster, they were all set for a big season.

As they started for the house, they saw Bess approaching at a run.

"Look!" she cried. "Here's an advance copy of Dad's book! They say it's going to be published in August!"

For several minutes Mark and Buck feasted their eyes on the novel. It had a handsome paper jacket with a picture of purple-blue mountains topped by white clouds. The title had been changed to *Lift Up Mine Eyes,* and they agreed it was probably an improvement.

"Golly," said Mark in awed tones. "Imagine—a real book with Dad's name on the cover! We'll have to give some of 'em for Christmas presents."

He was thinking of Jean as he said it and hoped afterward that the others hadn't guessed.

Mark had most of the work to do during the next week or so, for Buck was busy with preparations for the wedding. When the day dawned at last, it was fair and hot, as late June days often are in the mountains. Mark had borrowed a car to take his family down to the village church. As the hour approached, he grew fidgety. It seemed as if the final touches to Bess's wedding dress would never be finished. And he had his own hands full keeping the small fry clean and out of mischief.

At last they reached the church. The rest of the family were ushered to the front pews while Mark waited in the anteroom with Bess and one of her teacher friends who was acting as her maid of honor.

The soft organ music picked up volume with the first bars of the wedding march. Then, at the slow pace they had rehearsed, he moved down the aisle with the bride on his arm. He had never thought of Bess as an especially pretty girl, but now, in her white gown and veil, he saw that she was radiantly lovely.

Buck, looking stiff and solemn, stood with Joe Sullivan at the right of the altar. Mark relinquished his sister and stood aside, and the ceremony began. The sober words were read, the responses clearly given. Joe had the ring ready. After the groom slipped it on Bess's finger, the minister pronounced them man and wife, and it was all over. Mark drew a long breath of relief as the young couple went up the aisle, all smiles and blushes.

There was a reception afterward at the Grange Hall. Then, when all the neighbors had kissed the bride and the older women had had a good cry, Buck and Bess drove off in a shower of rice and old shoes. Mark watched them out of sight around the corner before he went back for more cake and strawberries and ice cream. He knew the bride and groom were headed for New York and Atlantic City, and their honeymoon would be a happy one. Weddings, he decided, were great things, but it was just as well they didn't happen every day.

Chapter 7

On Monday morning Mark was in the blueberry plantation early. As he had expected, the hot sun of the last three days had speeded up the ripening. Two acres of early bushes held berries ready to be gathered.

He hurried home in Buck's pickup truck and marshaled his forces. Elmer, Emily, Bill, and little Jane swarmed aboard, gleeful at the prospect of working and earning money. Mrs. Wilkins promised to come down as soon as her household tasks were done.

Mark gave each youngster a stack of quart boxes, lectured them on how to pick only ripe berries without damaging the green ones, then turned them loose. He kept the tally and carried the filled boxes to the truck, following the children down the rows.

Emily was the prize picker. She was twelve and had had years of experience at the job. Her agile fingers flew, and the huge berries piled up fast in her boxes. Elmer could match her in speed, but he didn't stick to it as steadily. At the end of the morning he had a count of ninety-five boxes, while Emily had picked a hundred and two. The younger ones were slower. Mark had to clean up the tops of the bushes, too high for their short arms to reach.

Mrs. Wilkins had brought a basket of lunch, which they ate in the shade of an elm tree on the lawn. Mark studied the tally sheet between bites of his sandwich.

"Almost three hundred an' fifty quarts," he announced. "Ought to hit better than six hundred for the day. If we can get the cellophane covers on, say, five hundred boxes, I'll take 'em over to Beaver Lake tomorrow."

His mother beamed. "At three cents a quart, that's more than ten dollars you children have earned this morning. I don't expect Bill and Janie to keep it up, but I'll pitch in and help. The Wilkins family may be rich yet!"

"Three cents is the rate when you're filling boxes," said Mark. "It'll be only two cents a pound when we start shipping to the freezer, but you'll be able to make about as much. Picking the berries into ten-quart pails, it'll go faster."

By five o'clock they had beaten the quota Mark had set. Six hundred and eighty quarts of fine big berries stood in rows on the long packing table. His mother took the smaller children home while Elmer and Emily stayed to help Mark put on the cellophane. And before it grew too dark to work, they had covered five hundred quarts.

Next morning he stacked the boxes in the truck, covered them carefully with a tarpaulin, and set off for Beaver Lake. The rest of the family remained behind to keep on picking. His first stop was at the big dining camp where many of the cottagers ate their meals. The woman in charge was an old friend of his, and she welcomed the news that Pocono Sky-Blues were on the market once more.

"I expect I could use fifty quarts," she said. "I s'pose they're the same price—forty cents, wholesale? That's what Buck always charged me. Seems high, but they're such beauties, I guess they're worth it."

Mark unloaded the berries. "Rather pay now?" he asked. "Or the end o' the month? I'll be coming in every few days, an' I'll keep account o' what you take."

She preferred to be billed by the month, so he wrote the amount down in the little notebook he carried. After a stop at the clubhouse to say hello to Mr. Ackroyd, he set out to make a round of the lake.

Now in late June the cottages were filling up. Canoes and sailboats were in evidence. Eight or ten young people were playing tennis, and an archery class was in progress on the field behind the clubhouse. A few hardy swimmers were braving the cold mountain water at the main dock.

At almost every occupied camp Mark sold a few quarts of berries. As he neared the Langleys' big rustic cottage, he saw the station wagon parked in the drive, and his heart began to beat faster. But when he went to the kitchen door, it was Mrs. Langley who answered his knock. She knew him at once and smiled a welcome.

"Those lovely big blueberries!" she exclaimed. "Ripe already! We just came up last night, and Jean's gone off with some friends on a woods hike to the falls. I'll tell her you were here—and I'd like two quarts of berries. Let's see—that's a dollar, isn't it?"

He took the money and thanked her. "I expect I'll be

'round again before the week's over," he said. "Maybe next time Jean'll be here."

By midafternoon he had sold four hundred boxes. With the rest he drove to Bonham's general store in the village. Mr. Bonham had a long-standing agreement with Buck and was glad to take the hundred quarts that remained, paying thirty-five cents a box.

"It's got so folks won't buy wild berries no more," he said. "They like the big fellers, an' they're willin' to pay twice as much to git 'em."

Mark carried a pocketful of bills and silver to the Evanses' house that night and locked the money up in Buck's safe. Mr. Evans was an invalid whose legs had been paralyzed for years. But he sat in a wheel chair and took a lively interest in the doings on the place.

"Must have had a good day with the berries," he said.

"That's right," Mark told him. "First o' the season, so everybody wanted some. I took in two hundred an' ten dollars, plus twenty on credit. Tomorrow I reckon I may take a load to the freezer if the kids have picked enough. No word from the newlyweds, I suppose?"

Mr. Evans chuckled. "We might get a post card by the end o' the week. They've got other things on their minds besides writing home. Anyhow, Buck knows everything's all right with you in charge."

After supper Mark went over the tally sheets with his mother. She showed him the figures for each of the four children.

"I had 'em wait till the dew was off," she said, "so as not to spoil the bloom on the berries. They picked two hundred more quarts in boxes, an' we got the cellophane on 'em. Then in the afternoon we started picking for the freezer an' filled six o' those big crates—fifty pounds apiece. There are about three more rows of the early berries, an' then we'll have to wait for new ones to ripen."

Mark was well satisfied. He wanted Buck to be pleased with the way he had handled things. Next morning he called the manager of the freezing plant from the Evanses' house. Yes, he was told, they would be ready to handle five hundred pounds any time he brought them in.

As soon as the morning dew was dry, he handed out buckets to the small fry and took two of them himself. By lunchtime they had filled four more crates. At one o'clock Mark loaded the truck and set off for Crow Ridge.

It was the first time he had visited the plant. The new concrete building that housed it was small but equipped with modern machinery, and everything looked immaculately clean. As fast as he carried the crates inside, the berries were weighed. The scale showed a total of five hundred and twenty pounds, and a hundred and four dollars were duly credited to Buck's account.

Rolled out on an endless rubber belt, the fruit now moved into a quick-freezing unit, where the temperature, Mark learned, was kept at a constant forty degrees below zero. At the end of three hours the berries, hard as bullets now, would be weighed into one-pound boxes, printed with the Pocono Sky-Blues brand, and put into the big storage freezer, where the temperature stayed at zero.

The manager explained all this, obviously proud to talk about his new equipment. "Yours are the first blueberries we've had," he told Mark. "They're certainly top quality—all Buck Evans said they'd be. I expect some of the other growers will be bringing in fruit soon. How long before you can let us have some more?"

The boy considered. "Well," he said, "we still have a few rows of early berries to pick, and after that we'll be going over 'em a second time. I might be able to bring down another five hundred pounds by Saturday. After that we'll have to wait for the next bunch of bushes to ripen. But Buck'll be home before that, an' you'd better discuss it with him. I know he promised you twenty thousand pounds for the whole season, an' from the way the bushes look now, I reckon you'll get 'em."

On Friday he took another truckload of berries to the colony at Beaver Lake. The weekly sailing race was getting under way, and as he passed the clubhouse, he saw a dozen cricket-class boats maneuvering for the start above the main dock. From the gunwale of the nearest one a brown-haired girl in a white jersey waved to him. It was Jean Langley, crewing for one of the local sailors. That, he thought, with some disappointment, was all he was likely to see of her. In that, however, he was wrong.

By going first to the other side of the lake, he postponed his visit to the Langleys' cottage until early afternoon. By then the race was over and Jean was at home, curled up in a swing on the porch.

"Hi!" she hailed him. "Mother said you hadn't been here yet, so I waited."

Grinning, Mark got out of the truck. "Some nice berries today, Ma'am?" he inquired, as businesslike as possible. "Fresh-picked Sky-Blues, big as the end o' your thumb!"

She laughed with him. "Bring two quarts," she said. "And then come up here and sit a while. You must be worn out. Have you had your lunch?"

"Oh, sure," he told her. It wasn't a real lie because earlier in the day he had eaten a piece of fresh-baked pie, offered him by the woman who ran the dining camp. He delivered the berries, then joined Jean on the porch.

"Now," she said, "I want to hear all that's been going on. Have you cleared the ski slope yet?"

"Just made a start, but it'll be ready before snow." He went on to explain how busy he had been with Buck away. Then he told her about the wedding. Of course she wanted to know just how the bride was dressed.

"I've never met your sister," she said, "but I know she must have looked beautiful."

Mark nodded. "I guess I never really thought about it till that day," he replied, "but Bess is a mighty pretty girl."

"And you finished your junior year at school, didn't you?" Jean went on. "Do you have any plans about going to college next year?"

"Yes," he answered. "But I know it won't be easy. If there's a chance, I'd like to try to get into Penn State. What about you?"

"Bryn Mawr, I hope," she said. "I know a Dartmouth man on the ski team, and he wants me to go to Middlebury, but I'd rather be nearer home."

Mark felt a twinge of jealousy toward Dartmouth men on the ski team. "I'm glad," he told her. "If you were up there in Vermont, you'd get all the skiing you want and never come near the Poconos."

"True enough," she said with a laugh. "Perhaps that's one reason I'd rather stay in Pennsylvania. Anyway, I don't have to make up my mind for a year."

Mark rose regretfully. "I've still got a couple of hundred boxes to sell," he said apologetically. "Next week I guess Buck'll be making the rounds. But if you should happen to be driving over our way, I'll show you the trail I've laid out. It's not quite as full o' turns as the 'Tail-Wagger' at Baird's Notch, but I think you'll like it."

* * *

The honeymooners returned on Sunday afternoon, looking tanned and happy. As soon as Buck had unpacked, he went down to the berry plantation with Mark and looked over the situation.

"I sure picked a fine time to go off, didn't I?" He chuckled. "I never dreamed those Pioneers would ripen so fast. But you've done everything needed at least as well as I could. Boy, look at those next bushes! Really loaded, aren't they?"

There came a week in mid-July when the early-bearing

berries had all been picked and the next lot hadn't quite ripened. The haying, too, was done.

"What say we finish that stump-pulling job?" suggested Buck, and Mark, of course, was delighted.

With Elmer's help they worked steadily, going higher and higher up the slope. Several times they drilled big boulders and split them with dynamite, using the tractor to haul away half-ton fragments. In four days they had the whole trail cleared and the stumps piled, ready to be burned.

"The weather's treated us fine so far," Buck remarked, wiping his sweaty face with a bandanna. "Now it looks like rain tomorrow. Tonight ought to be a good time for our bonfire."

Mark looked at the thirty-foot pyramid of stumps and grinned. "It'll sure make a humdinger!" he said. "Probably have the whole village up here when they see it."

"That's right, and we don't want to scare 'em. I have to go to the store before supper, an' I'll spread the word so folks won't think it's a house burning."

Well before dusk Mark had the youngsters shove dry kindling under the edges of the pile. Then he ordered them all to stand back while he poured on kerosene. Finally he lighted a match, tossed it into the kindling, and ran.

The result was even more spectacular than he had foreseen. With a gathering roar the flames shot upward through the mass of dry roots. When most of the wood was burning, the blaze went up fifty feet or more, lighting the whole sky. And the heat was so intense that the young Wilkinses were glad to stand well away.

Mark looked toward the road and saw a dozen cars already stopped there to watch. More came every moment. Fortunately the stumps had been piled at a safe distance from the woods, and there was little wind to carry the sparks. Even so, the chief of the Crow Ridge Volunteer Fire Company stood anxiously by, ready to call for the chemical truck if the blaze got out of hand. He was there at Buck's request.

The fire burned for two hours, and before it had died down, practically everybody on the mountain had come to see it. Mark, his face blackened by smoke and charred wood, raced around the pile beating out sparks with a shovel. Suddenly, as he stopped to catch his breath, he heard a laugh beside him.

"If you aren't a sight!" said Jean Langley. "We saw the glow in the sky and came rushing over. I thought surely you'd been burned out."

"It had me scared myself for a bit," he told her with a sooty grin. "But I guess it's safe enough now. Come on—let's see if we can find my sister and Buck."

Bess, it turned out, was easily found. When the throng began to gather, she had made two big pails of lemonade, and now she was passing out paper cups of it to friends and neighbors.

When Mark and Jean approached, she turned over the dispensing of refreshments to her smaller sisters. "Welcome to the party!" she called cheerily. "Who'd ever have thought that burning a few stumps would turn into a bigger affair than a covered-dish supper at the church!"

In a moment the two girls were chatting as if they had known each other for years. Proud of them both, Mark picked up his shovel again and went back to keep an eye on what was left of the fire. And then, as if it had waited for the last stump to be consumed, the rain fell.

Chapter 8

Mark counted up his savings and found he had more than two hundred dollars. It was enough, he decided, to make at least a start on the little "lodge" he wanted to build at the foot of the slope. Borrowing Buck's truck, he went down to the Crow Ridge lumberyard.

New lumber, he soon discovered, would cost more than he could afford to spend. But at the back of the yard there were a few piles of used boards and timbers. Some were weathered gray and showed nailholes, but for the most part they were sound enough. He got the list of what he needed out of his pocket and began selecting pieces. For corner posts he took four-by-sixes, and for sills and stringers and a ridgepole he bought two-by-six planks. Then he got light two-by-four studding. Rough one-inch boards for roof and siding were easy to find, and as he meant to cover the outside with slabs, he cared little about how they looked.

The total so far came to ninety dollars, but he spent thirty more on asphalt shingles, for he wanted a good tight roof. After that, thirty dollars went for door and window frames and several sizes of nails. He still had about sixty dollars remaining.

The rough plan he had drawn called for a floor measurement of twenty feet by twelve. That would give him room for an oil-burning range, storage cupboards, and a counter at one end. The rest of the space would do for people to come in and get warm, eat their sandwiches, and sip their coffee or soft drinks. There would be no cellar, of course. The floor would be concrete slab, poured right on the ground.

That afternoon Mark leveled the site where the building would stand. With some old boards from the Wilkinses' barn, he measured and built foot-high forms, enclosing the rectangle. Then he called up a company in Stroudsburg that dealt in ready-mix concrete. They agreed to haul in and pour the eight cubic yards he needed next day, and the cost would be just what he had left—sixty dollars. He drew a long breath and told them to go ahead and deliver it. Even though it left him broke, he had to have faith in his ability to finish the job.

With Elmer's help he trued up the vertical posts that evening, setting four in the corners of the form and two more midway between the ends. Promptly at ten o'clock the next morning the huge yellow mixer-truck rolled up the highway and stopped in front of the projected building. The foreman checked on Mark's grading with a big spirit level.

"Made a pretty good job of it," he commented. "A couple o' shovelfuls o' dirt in this corner an' she'll do. I can back in across the ditch here an' pour right into your form. What we've got in the drum ought to give you about a ten-inch slab."

Within half an hour the pouring and spreading were completed. The smooth surface of gray cement shone wetly in the sun. Proudly Mark handed over the money and the truck departed.

"Gosh!" said Elmer. "Sure looks pretty, doesn't it?"

Mark nodded. "So pretty," he replied, "it's a temptation to wade in it. One of us'll have to stand guard till it sets, or kids an' dogs'll be making tracks all over the place."

It was just as well they kept watch. First Buck Evans' old hound Tige came sniffing up to investigate. Then little Bill Wilkins was grabbed by the seat of his pants just in time to prevent a catastrophe. That night Mark spread hay over the rapidly drying surface and laid some boards crisscross to discourage prowlers.

By morning the slab was firm enough, but they decided to leave a protective covering over it for one more day. Meanwhile, another variety of blueberries had ripened, and all hands had to go back to work.

For two weeks Mark was too busy to make much progress on the little structure. But in the evenings, with help from Elmer, he did manage to complete the framing and set the ridgepole. Gradually he was accumulating a little more money.

"Hey," said his younger brother one evening. "Know what would look nice? A stone fireplace here on the end."

"I know," Mark answered regretfully. "I thought of it, too. But the cheapest I could get a mason to build it would be eight or nine hundred dollars. An' if we tried to do it ourselves, the chances are it wouldn't draw right. There's a real trick to building a flue."

Picking and marketing berries went on steadily through the rest of July and most of August. Buck and Bess were happy over the bumper crop. At the rate they were going, they could expect to clear six or seven thousand dollars for the season, and already Buck was planning to increase his acreage and order more plants from New Jersey. At the same time he was still paying the small Wilkinses to locate wild bushes with especially big berries. Crossing the two strains had proved to be a real success.

Late one afternoon, as Mark was coming home from

work, he saw a slight figure in overalls racing down out of the woods. It was his sister Emily. She reached his side pale and panting, her eyes wide with fright.

"There was a—a man," she gasped, "an' he had a gun! I've been running all the way home."

Mark put his arm around her thin shoulders. "Steady, now, Sis," he said. "Where was this? An' who was the man?"

She was still trembling with terror, but she did her best to tell him. "I was looking for berry bushes," she explained. "Way over the mountain, on the other side o' the swamp. I'd never been that far before. All of a sudden he came out o' the brush an' he looked—awful! A dark beard all over his face, an' ragged clothes and an old hat pulled down over his eyes!"

"The gun," Mark said, shaking her arm. "What was it—a revolver?"

"No, a big gun—a rifle, I think. He pointed it right at me an' said if I wasn't out o' there before he counted three, he'd kill me! I didn't wait to hear him count. I just ran—an' I've been running ever since!"

"All right, Sis," Mark told her gently. "You're home now, an' nobody's going to hurt you."

He took her into the house and let his mother comfort her. Then he went down to Buck's and telephoned the state police. It was Sergeant Green who answered.

"Hmm," he said when he had heard Mark's story. "Sounds like that deer poacher that Warden Jones has been after. Can your sister give us a good description? Maybe I'd better drive up there an' talk to her."

He arrived after supper, questioned the girl, and made a rough map of the area where she had seen the man.

"I'll go up in daylight tomorrow," he said, "an' have a look around. Meanwhile, I guess you'd better keep the kids on this side o' the mountain."

They learned later that the sergeant and two patrolmen had scoured the ridge beyond the swamp and found no trace of the man with the rifle. For the time being, that seemed to be the last of the affair.

* * *

Mark was glad to have a good summer job with his brother-in-law, but it was discouraging that he couldn't make faster progress on the ski lodge. Labor Day was almost upon them, and right after that school would be starting.

Buck called him aside one evening. "You aren't planning to go off anywhere over Labor Day, are you?" he asked.

"Me?" said Mark. "Where'd I go—an' how? No, I'll be right here, sawing boards an' driving nails, I reckon."

Buck grinned mysteriously. "O.K.," he said. "I just wondered, that's all. I should ha' known you'd want to work on the lodge."

It rained part of that week, but the Saturday before Labor Day was bright and clear. Mark hurried through his chores. Then he gathered his carpenter's tools and started out of the yard. Elmer and the other children had already disappeared.

"Wait a minute, Son," his mother called after him. "I think I'll go down with you."

He stood there impatiently till she came out, carrying an immense covered basket. It must be something she was taking to Bess, he thought. Shifting his tools to his left hand, he hoisted the basket up on his shoulder and they set off down the road.

As soon as they came in sight of the cutover land, Mark stopped suddenly, his mouth hanging open. Drawn up there along the highway were eight or ten cars, and the place seemed to be swarming with people. His mother began to laugh.

"Don't look so flabbergasted, Mark." She chuckled. "It's a surprise—sort of a barn-raising. Buck got the neighbors together. You never knew a thing about it, did you?"

"No," said he, "I sure didn't. What have you got in this basket, anyhow?"

"Doughnuts," she told him. "A hundred an' twenty of 'em I made yesterday. Bess is bringing the coffee. We figured the crowd might get hungry before the job's all done."

In the group standing around the framework of the building Mark recognized high-school friends, neighboring farmers, and even a few young businessmen from Crow Ridge. Buck was there, of course, and he saw Joe Sullivan. Everybody was laughing, talking, and having a good time.

"Here's the boss, boys!" someone yelled. "Come on, Mark—show us what you want done."

He was still almost speechless, but he managed to greet those he knew best. Then, awkwardly, he spread out his pencil-drawn plan and tried to explain what he had meant to do next.

"The door goes here," he said, "an' the windows at each end an' the back. Then the siding has to be nailed on an' covered with tar paper. I aim to put slabs on over that. The packs o' shingles there are for the roof."

"O.K.!" Buck yelled. "Let's go!"

Most of the men and boys had brought their own tools, and all of them knew how to saw to a line and drive a nail straight. Mark did his best to help, but he was pushed good-naturedly out of the way.

"Just give the orders," Moose Martin told him. "We'll do the work."

It went amazingly fast. By noon the siding was up and the door and window frames installed. They ate in relays in the Evans kitchen, with Bess serving while her

mother and mother-in-law did the cooking. The doughnuts had long since disappeared.

There wasn't room for all the men to work on the roof at the same time, so after the tar paper had been nailed on, most of the helpers stood around swapping yarns. At four o'clock the job was completed—walls solid and a tight roof overhead.

Mark beat on the head of a nail keg with his hammer and got their attention.

"Never knew I had so many friends," he said. "All I can do is thank you all an' give you an invitation. The day the first good snow comes, I'll expect you up here to try the slope. Everybody who's helped with the job today gets to ski free."

They laughed and cheered and slapped him on the back. "I ain't been on skis fer twenty years," said one middle-aged farmer. "But by gum, I'll come an' take ye up on that!"

Soon they were starting up their cars and waving good-by. As the last ones departed, another car drove up—a big, shiny station wagon. In it was Jean Langley, alone. She got out and came over to join Mark and his family.

"I heard about the 'bee' from Mr. Ackroyd," she said. "But I certainly didn't expect to see the place all finished! May I look inside?"

Proudly Mark showed her the interior. "When these shavings an' loose nails are swept up," he said, "it'll look a little better. I aim to build a sort of lunch counter over here, with an oilstove to cook on. If that doesn't keep the place warm enough, I can get a space heater for the other end. An' maybe I'll throw together a few benches to put along the walls. It's nothing fancy—just a place to rest an' have something to eat. Come on up the hill a little way. I want to show you the trail we cleared."

From halfway up the slope the outline of the trail was clearly visible. Jean was enthusiastic.

"Honestly," she told him, "I like this as well as anything at Baird's Notch. And I never did mind climbing. Just get some good snow on it, and you'll see me up here!"

* * *

Before school started, Mark borrowed the pickup truck once more and drove to a portable sawmill, operating over on the Bear Creek road. It was the same company that had logged the Wilkinses' cutover land. Mark was acquainted with the foreman and found him a sympathetic listener when he explained why he wanted to buy slabs.

"We've got plenty of 'em," said the foreman. "Use 'em for fuel for the boiler an' the cookhouse. But if you want slabs to make your building look like a log cabin, you ought to have 'em edged. That way they'll set snug. I could pick out enough good hemlock slabs for what you need an' run 'em through the edger for only a couple o' bucks extra. The whole thing won't cost you more'n twenty dollars. What length do you want 'em?"

"Twelve feet," said Mark. "That's long enough for the ends, an' I can cut an' fit for the back an' front."

"They'll be ready tomorrow," the foreman promised.

Mark returned next day, and by careful roping succeeded in getting the whole load aboard the truck. Even from inside the cab he could catch the fresh, woodsy smell of hemlock as he drove homeward. He piled the slabs neatly beside the lodge and took the pickup back to Buck's. As he drove into the yard, he saw a car parked by the door and recognized it as the one owned by the game warden, Dick Jones.

In the kitchen the warden was talking to Buck. He turned to Mark as the boy came in.

"Heard any guns being fired at night lately?" he asked.

"No," said Mark. "Not that I can remember."

"There's a rumor around," Jones explained, "that somebody's been jack-lighting deer again. I wouldn't be surprised if it's the same bushy-bearded fellow that scared your sister."

Mark nodded. "That's likely," he said. "But the place she ran into him was two or three miles away, on the other side o' the mountain. I doubt if we could hear a shot from that far, at our house."

"Well," the warden said with a shrug, "I've already spent two nights in the woods up there without catching him. Let me know if you do hear anything. Evans, here, knows my number."

Chapter 9

There was fall work to be done in the blueberry plantation, and Mark helped Buck with it on weekends. In such spare time as they could find, he and Elmer nailed slabs on the walls of the lodge. The edging had been a good idea. The straight sides of the slabs fitted together neatly and the final effect, if one didn't look too closely, was that of a well-built log house.

More and more people on the mountain were having electricity put in that fall. Watching the utility men run lines to various farmhouses, Mark had an idea. He called at the home of a neighbor where electric power was being installed and asked about a used cookstove.

The farmer had just bought a new electric range. He was delighted to get rid of the old oil cooker that had been put out in the barn, and Mark bought it for only three dollars. Once he had cleaned it up and scoured away all the rust, his mother assured him it would do perfectly for heating soup, hot dogs, and coffee at the ski lodge. There was even a removable top like a hot plate, on which pancakes could be cooked.

The counter and benches would have to wait until football season was over. Mark practiced with the team every afternoon. He had been a reserve back for two years and now found himself promoted to first-string quarterback.

Coach Winton didn't give them too many plays. With

a small squad and few available replacements, he knew he had to keep the boys in good physical condition. So he had them concentrate on fundamentals—hard blocking, solid tackling, and sure control of the ball. Most of the plays were run from a straight T-formation, with Mark handing off or keeping. He had a couple of tall, fast ends who could catch passes, and though the line lacked weight, it charged hard. Moose Martin, the biggest man on the team, played fullback. At the two halves were Joe Rossi and Rudy Bender.

They played Stroudsburg in their first game and took a beating from the larger school. That was expected. But the fact that they lost by only ten points, 24 to 14, gave them encouragement. They had a breather against Bear Creek and won, 27 to 12. Then came the game they really wanted to win. In football Mt. Pocono had always been their traditional rival.

The game was at Crow Ridge this year. All through Saturday morning the cars drifted in from the backwoods settlements, and by two o'clock the wooden stands overflowed with more than a thousand spectators. Even at Stroudsburg the turnout had been only a few more. Mark took a long breath of the crisp October air and wondered if all the other players were as tense as he was. Then they trotted out for a few warm-up plays, and with the exercise the knot in his stomach began to relax. He was feeling fine at kick-off time.

Crow Ridge had won the toss and chosen to receive. The ball sailed toward Joe Rossi, who caught it on the run. Mark cut across in time to block the first man downfield, and Joe sped up the sideline for twenty yards before he was tackled. From the thirty-five, Moose went over tackle for a four-yard gain. Then, in the huddle, Mark called for a long pass.

He faked a hand-off to the plunging Moose, cut back

with the ball hidden, and dodged two linemen. Off to the left he could spot Link Freeman sprinting upfield. He cocked his arm and threw a long, clean spiral, trying to lead the end by a stride. And as it left his fingers, he was smothered under a rush of tacklers. Not till he regained his feet did he know what had happened. His teammates were jumping up and down, and Sam Bonham pounded him on the back. Link had taken the pass and run for a touchdown.

As they huddled before the conversion, Moose Martin got his ear. "Let's go for the two-pointer," he was whispering. "They'll think we're going to pass. Just give it to me—if I can't make the yardage through that line, I'll eat the football!"

The two teams lined up, and as soon as it was obvious that there would be no place kick, Mark saw the opposing line-backers drop back to block a pass. Moose had guessed right. Mark leaned low behind the center's buttocks, took the snap, and whirled, slapping the ball into the big fullback's middle. In the same motion he leaped up, arm raised as if to throw. Moose hit the line like a bulldozer. When the pile untangled, he was over by a foot.

That eight-point advantage stood up through the first quarter. Then, on sheer power plays, Mt. Pocono drove for a touchdown. Trying to even the score, they threw a jump pass over the line on the conversion, and Mark's leaping stab at the ball knocked it clear of the receiver's hands. The half ended with Crow Ridge still ahead, 8 to 6.

Coach Winton looked serious as he faced his team between the halves. "They've got more substitutes than we have," he said. "Some of you are going to be mighty tired before it's over, for you'll have to play the whole game. So I think our best bet is to go for another score quick, while you're fresh. We'll be kicking off, but we've got to get that ball before they can start rolling again."

Years earlier the Crow Ridge squad had played in ancient, tattered uniforms and were known as the Scarecrows. The nickname had stuck. Mt. Pocono even had a derisive cheer that went "Scarecrows! Scarecrows! Where'd ya get the ol' clo'es?"

They were yelling it now, as the eleven lined up to kick. Moose's toe hit the ball squarely and sent it booming nearly to the goal line. Instead of letting it roll across, an ambitious halfback picked it up and tried for a runback. Link Freeman smashed through the interference and nailed him inside the ten. It was a jarring tackle, but the back managed to hang on to the ball. Two tries at the line were stopped by vicious charging and produced only four yards.

"Will they pass on third down?" Mark wondered to himself, and started backpedaling to be ready. Then the ball was snapped, and he realized suddenly that it wasn't a pass—it was a quick kick!

At top speed he sprinted back. A hasty glance over his shoulder showed him the ball in the air, wobbling in his direction. He whirled and caught it on the enemy forty-yard line. There were a lot of Mt. Pocono men racing down on him and no blockers in sight.

Mark darted to his left, swiveled, and avoided the first tackler, straight-armed the second. There was a little daylight ahead of him now. He angled toward the sideline, trying to give his teammates time to form some interference. Moose was the first to make it. The big fullback threw his body across the path of the two nearest opponents, taking them both out. And, running like a scalded cat, Mark cut through the hole. Yard stripes were blurring past under his feet. The safety man made a desperate dive at his legs and missed. Then there were no more white markers. He was in the end zone.

They scored another two-point conversion with Bender skirting right end. After that the game settled down to bruising, bone-rattling ground plays. The Scarecrows hung on grimly until midway in the fourth quarter. Then Mt. Pocono, with half a dozen fresh players in the line-up, ground out another touchdown. Their place kicker came in and put the extra point over the crossbar.

Receiving the kickoff, Mark used Moose Martin in three straight plays to get a first down. Strong as he was, the fullback was gasping with weariness when he got up, and Mark knew he would have to rest him. On the next play he faked the ball to Rossi, ran back as if to throw, then carried it himself. The opposing forwards were caught off balance, and he was able to slip past them for a dozen yards and another first down. The tackle was a rough one, knocking the wind out of him. Coach Winton called for a time out.

The two-minute rest seemed all too short, for the whole

Crow Ridge team was so bushed that they could hardly stand. But somehow, by sheer bulldog determination, they held on to the ball through one more series of downs. With a minute and a half left, they had to kick from their own forty-seven. Moose angled the punt beautifully. It bounced once in the corner, then rolled out of bounds on the two-yard line. And before Mt. Pocono could get it past midfield, the final gun sounded.

Bone-weary, the Scarecrows staggered off the field into the arms of their howling admirers. They had won by a score of 16 to 13.

* * *

The football season was over for Crow Ridge by the middle of November. They dropped one more game, to a tough team from the coal-mining area near Scranton, but wound up with a record of five wins and only two defeats.

There was a football dance in the school gymnasium the Friday night before Thanksgiving. Mark rode down with Buck and Bess, and before they pulled into the parking lot, the first snow of the winter had begun to fall.

"If this keeps up," his brother-in-law remarked, "you'll have skiing on that slope of yours before you know it."

Mark looked at the big flakes blowing out of the north and agreed. Inside the gym a dozen of his friends crowded around him.

"Think we can come an' ski tomorrow?" they asked.

He laughed. "As soon as there's enough snow, you can all come," he told them. "But you'd better wait an' see how much we get out o' this one. Wouldn't want you to try it till there's at least a foot."

The snow was still coming down steadily when they drove home at midnight, and nearly six inches had already accumulated. On Saturday morning Mark looked out on a white world. The storm showed no sign of ending, and the wind had risen. He could hardly see the barn through the driving flakes. There would be no skiing in such weather. He shoveled out a path and did the chores, then came in to breakfast.

"Can we try the slope?" Elmer asked eagerly, but Mark shook his head.

"Not a chance today, I'm afraid," he answered. "You couldn't even see the trail. Tell you what, though. There's some lumber in the barn, an' we can start building those benches for the lodge."

Working most of the day, they finished two of them and made a start on the counter, as well. By three o'clock it was too dark to see, even by lantern light. The snow was still drifting, and they had to shovel out again to get back to the house.

"Gosh!" said Elmer ruefully. "I was prayin' for snow! Guess I must have prayed too hard."

Mark chuckled as he answered. "Never mind," he said. "Once this is over, we'll have skiing—and how!"

The storm ended in the night, and when Sunday's sun came up, it shone on huge billows of glistening white. Mark bounded out of bed and pulled the covers off his brother. "Come on!" he urged. "Get the work done an' we'll go!"

Not much more than an hour later they were putting on their skis. Deep as the snow was, it was packed firmly enough to bear their weight. They cut straight across through the woods to the upper part of the ski slope.

"Boy—look at that!" cried Elmer. "Smooth as a roof!"

They climbed all the way to the top and looked down at the bends of the trail. From here it somehow appeared narrower and more twisting than it had in the summer.

"Better let me go first," said Mark. "Swinging around that first big ledge may be tricky."

Two seconds after the start he was moving fast, and

he took the sharp curve to the left with a jump turn. There was a quick drop past the end of the bare, windswept ledge, then another bend to the right, where he came within a dozen feet of the trees. After that it was easier—a smooth turn left again and a long schuss that took him halfway down. He stemmed to a stop there and looked back.

Elmer had already started, a dark dot against the snow. He negotiated the first turn, shot down the drop, and made a frantic try to swing right again. Then he disappeared in a cloud of snow, one ski thrust high in the air.

Mark climbed the slope as fast as he could. It was a full minute before Elmer gave any sign of life. Then Mark saw him floundering, trying to get up. He was right in the edge of the woods. He looked as if he might be hurt, and Mark herringboned upward, panting a prayer. When he finally reached him, Elmer was sitting forlornly by the side of the trail.

"What happened?" called Mark. "Did you bust a leg?"

"Naw," the youngster replied with disgust. "It's one o' my skis!"

He explained then. After the drop he knew he was going too fast, and the woods were so close that he saw he couldn't make it. So he had thrown himself sidewise in the snow. His left ski hit the trunk of a tree and splintered, but by luck his ankle wasn't broken.

"It hurts enough," he said, "but I can move it, so I'm pretty sure it's no more'n a sprain."

"I'm sorry," said Mark. "It's my fault for laying out the trail wrong. First, we've got to get you home an' see to that ankle. Then I'll bring an ax up here an' cut some brush to block off that upper part. Anybody who wants to ski will just have to start below the ledge."

They tied the broken ski beside the sound one, and Elmer sat on the narrow toboggan they formed. Holding on to a ski pole, he was towed down the hill and home. As they neared the dooryard, he got off.

"Ma'll think I'm killed," he muttered, hobbling thigh-deep through the drifts.

She had indeed seen them coming and flown to the door expecting the worst. Her relief at the sight of Elmer on his feet was so great that she didn't even scold him. In a few minutes she had him sitting in a kitchen chair, his swollen ankle soaking in hot water and Epsom salts.

Mark told her why he had to go back to the slope. "There may be some folks coming to ski," he said, "and most of 'em won't be as good at it as Elmer. I'll have to keep 'em off that part o' the trail."

He got an ax and climbed the hill again. There were enough young trees showing above the snow so that he had no trouble cutting tops for a barricade. It was only when he had finished and looked down the hill that he realized these precautions were hardly needed. The highway at the foot was still deeply drifted. Not a car had been through, and there was no sign of the state plows. Blueberry Mountain would stay cut off from the outside world for another day at least.

Mark frowned, then gave a chuckle. It seemed ironic enough that the first snow—so eagerly awaited—had been too heavy for any skiers to visit the slope. He found a piece of cord in his jacket pocket and used it to tie the ax behind his shoulders. Then he picked up the ski poles. At least there was no reason why he shouldn't enjoy a run by himself.

Just as he started to shove off, a sound reached his ears. It was the faint, far-off crack of a rifle, muffled by distance.

Chapter 10

Mark straightened up, frozen to attention. He listened for half a minute and heard the sound again. There was no question about it this time. The rifle shots he had heard came from the other side of the mountain, somewhere beyond the swamp. And that was where Emily had encountered the bearded man.

Deer season wouldn't open until after Thanksgiving, and he was sure this shooting was to kill deer. He had better get down to Buck's and call the game warden on the telephone. Then he remembered. The roads were still blocked, and the warden wouldn't be able to get through.

For a moment he stood there undecided. If he went home for his rifle, he would waste half an hour and the poacher might be a long way off by the time he got back. It was probably dangerous to go after him unarmed, but he was willing to take the risk if he could get a glimpse of the man. Resolutely he turned and went over the shoulder of the mountain.

There had been little drifting among the trees. The snow lay deep and level, and the hemlock branches were heavy with masses of white. Mark skied steadily ahead through the woods, his ears straining to catch any sound in the distance. After a while he came to the edge of the swamp, where the trees were more open. Half a mile beyond he could make out the rugged crest of the ridge, shaggy with evergreens. From there he could probably be seen crossing the swamp, so he swung to the left and stayed in the shelter of the woods.

It was a good thing that he did. A few minutes later he glanced to his right across the swamp and saw something moving. At first he thought it was a deer. Then, stooping for a better view through the trees, he made out the head and body of a man. The figure was bending over some object in the snow. Soon he straightened up and swung the carcass of a buck deer over his shoulder. It was a heavy load, and he went slowly as he moved off toward the ridge, his rifle carried in his left hand.

At that distance Mark had been unable to see whether the man wore a beard, but he meant to get nearer and find out if possible. At least he thought he could identify the rough gray jacket and earlapped fur cap if he ever saw them again.

Staying in the cover of the trees the boy went forward, gaining a little and keeping the man in sight. Evidently he was on snowshoes, but even so he seemed to sink deep at every stride.

Mark was perhaps a hundred yards behind when the figure disappeared over the ridge. He hurried a little faster, following the snowshoe trail. And in his haste he didn't stop to reconnoiter before topping the crest. Suddenly something whined viciously past his ear, and he heard the heavy *whang* of a rifle.

Scared now, Mark dropped to his hands and knees where he would be out of sight. But he had already been seen. From down the slope on the other side came a harsh voice.

"Git back out o' there!" it called. "Git out an' make tracks. Show yerself jest once more an' you're a dead 'un!"

The voice sounded much nearer than Mark had ex-

pected. The poacher must have doubled back to watch his back trail. At any rate, the boy didn't wait to find out. He swung his skis around, still crouching low, and went down the hill the way he had come, speeding himself along with the poles. Not until he had put several hundred yards between himself and the ridge did he dare look over his shoulder. If the man was still there, he was well hidden. All Mark could see was the line of snow-laden hemlocks, silent and forbidding.

All the way home he raged at himself. He had thought he was a good woodsman, but he hadn't had sense enough to stay out of sight. By that piece of stupidity he had lost his chance to find out where the poacher was heading. Even if he had gone back for his rifle, he knew he would have been a fool to try shooting it out with the hard-voiced stranger.

Still fuming inwardly, he came to the upper end of the slope and schussed down with a rush. From the little lodge, now buried up to its window sills, it was only a short distance to the Evans farm. Buck was out shoveling paths to the barn and henhouse.

"Hi, boy!" he greeted Mark. "Won't get many ski fans out today, I guess. What are you looking so glum about?"

Briefly, Mark told him. "It was my own dumb fault," he finished. "If I'd had as much sense as a jaybird, the guy'd never have spotted me."

"Maybe," Buck replied. "In that business, I bet he watches his back trail pretty close, though. An' once he started shooting, there wasn't much you could do but beat it. Want to phone Dick Jones an' tell him?"

Mark's call found the warden at home. He heard the story out in silence. "Thanks for letting me know," he said at length. "That backs up my theory. Too bad you couldn't find out where he took the deer, but at least we're sure now where he's been operating. Soon as the road's open, I'll get you to take me up there. I'll bring a pair o' snowshoes."

It was past noon by then and Mark went home. In the kitchen the family was eating dinner. Elmer had his ankle bandaged and said it felt better.

Mark was able to laugh at his experience now. "Well, Emily," he told his young sister, "I've joined your club. That fellow with the rifle seems to have it in for us Wilkinses. Only this time he took a sure-enough shot at me."

"I think it's outrageous!" Mrs. Wilkins stormed. "What's this part o' the country coming to? Aren't the state troopers going to do something about it?"

"I couldn't tell you, Mom," Mark said with a grin. "All I did was call the game warden. Sometime, though, I'm going to find out who it was if it takes all winter."

The plows got through late that afternoon, and a few cars began to roll once more on the highway. During the night it snowed again. It had stopped by morning, but four or five more inches had fallen. Down at the road, Mark and his brothers and sisters waited for the school bus to take them to Crow Ridge.

As they stood there talking, a battered jeep panel truck went rattling past. Mark glanced up in time to be almost certain it was the same vehicle he had noticed once before —gray-painted, with no name and a license plate either missing or so dirty that it couldn't be read. This time it was headed down the mountain. He wished he had been able to see the driver.

That day the coach issued his first call for basketball. Mark wanted to play, of course, and after his last class he went to the bulletin board in the hall to sign up. Then, as he put the pencil back in his pocket, he saw two men waiting by the door. One of them he recognized at once as Dick Jones, the game warden. The other wore the trim gray uniform of the state police. Jones beckoned to him.

"Get your things on, Mark," the warden said. "We want you to come and guide us. I reckon you're acquainted with Sergeant Green?"

The sergeant was a sturdy six-footer with a strong square face. He shook hands with Mark, and when the boy had hustled into his outer clothes, they went at once to the warden's car. Mark was glad to see two pairs of snowshoes in the rear seat.

"You'd better tell us the story again," Jones suggested. "The sergeant may want to ask you some questions."

Without wasting words, Mark described what had happened the day before. "I'm not sure he aimed to hit me," he concluded, "but the shot came mighty close, so I didn't hang around to see any more."

Green nodded. "You were right," he said. "The fellow sounds dangerous. Can you describe him?"

"He didn't show his face. When I first saw him, he was bending over to pick up the deer, an' his back was toward me. But I'd say he was medium height and stocky. He had on a beat-up-looking gray Mackinaw or jacket an' a mangy fur cap with the flaps down."

As they neared the Wilkins place, Mark remembered the old jeep he had seen that morning. He asked the sergeant if he knew who owned it.

"No," said Green. "I've wondered about that myself. I met a jeep panel truck on the road the night before the blizzard. Guess it was the same one—gray, with the body scratched up as if it had gone through brush. It was near dusk, but he didn't have his lights on, so I couldn't see his rear plate. Then a couple of other cars came along, and before I could make a turn to follow him, he'd disappeared. Maybe pulled off on a woods road. Why? You think it might be our poacher friend?"

"I just wondered," said Mark. "Seems to me if he's killing deer for market, he'd have to have some way to get the meat out where he could sell it."

They parked in the edge of a drift, and the two men put on their snowshoes. Mark plowed his way to the house and got his own webs, deciding to use them instead of skis. He stopped long enough to tell his mother where he was going, then joined the others in the yard.

They climbed through the woods, angling across to the top of the ski slope. There Mark led the way over the mountain. He looked in vain for any trace of the ski tracks he had made yesterday. The new snow had covered them completely.

"Looks as if we won't be able to find his trail," he told the warden. "But I can show you where he killed the buck."

A mile or so farther on he pointed to a clump of jack pines at the edge of the swamp. "I was passing here when I first spotted him," he said. "He was right over that way."

They cut across the open expanse of white and came to a faint depression in the snow. Mark knelt, digging with his mittened hands. In a moment he uncovered a reddish patch four inches below the surface.

"Blood, all right," said Green. "Now—where'd he go from here?"

"That way," Mark told him. "Straight for the ridge."

The warden shielded his eyes, looking westward into the sun. "All right," he said. "Let's go. But we'd better watch the woods over there and spread out. We're a fine target, here in the open."

Cautiously they moved forward into the trees and up the slope. Just below the crest, Mark motioned for a halt.

"I'd gone about ten more steps," he whispered, "an' stuck my head over the top when he fired."

Green nodded. He crouched so low that he was practically crawling when he got to the crown of the ridge. After a careful scrutiny of the woods beyond, he beckoned them on. In silence they moved down the steep western slope. The ground was rough and rocky, with naked ledges thrusting through the snow. But search as they might, they found no snowshoe tracks. Last night's blanket had covered every sign.

Green straightened up with a scowl. "Well," he said, "he must have gone somewhere down this side. Maybe he's got a shack here in the woods."

He led the way along the edge of a deep, narrow ravine. Its bottom was clogged with a jungle of laurel and rhododendron, but they could see there was nothing like a house down there. The sun was behind the woods now, and dark shadows began to fall.

"Might as well follow the ravine down," Jones said. "Can't be more'n a mile to the Bear Creek road from here, an' that may be how he gets in an' out."

Mark knew they would be caught by darkness if they returned the way they had come. He hoped the warden was right about the direction they were taking. For the next ten minutes the three moved in single file along the side of the ravine. Jones was in the lead now, his eyes constantly covering the snow around him. Suddenly he stopped, pointing to the right.

"There's been a car parked here," he said. "Tracks lead out that way."

They examined the deep depressions in the snow, but they had filled in so that no tire marks were visible.

"Must have had plenty o' power an' traction to pull through this," Green remarked. "Looks more an' more as if it was that four-wheel-drive jeep."

A quarter of a mile farther on, still following the deep wheel ruts, they came in sight of a road. Mark recognized the place. They were on a narrow woods track he had seen once or twice before, and it was the Bear Creek road that lay just ahead.

Green looked up and down the narrow highway, then knelt down and undid the thongs of his snowshoes. "No point in waiting here," he growled. "The man we're after may not come back at all tonight. Let's hike on down till we find a telephone."

They had been walking only a minute or two when the lights of a car came over the hill behind them. The police sergeant stepped out into the road and held up his hand, and at the sight of his uniform the driver pulled quickly to a stop.

"We need a ride to the nearest house with a phone," Green explained. A moment later all three of them were in the car, and before they had ridden a mile, they spotted a farmhouse with wires running in. There the sergeant called the barracks and had a police car sent to pick them up. When they reached Mark's house, Green turned to him with a grin.

"You've been a big help," he said. "Didn't catch him this time, but don't worry—we will. Every trooper in the district will be watching for that jeep and keeping an eye on the woods road."

Mark did the milking, fed the animals, and came in to get his own supper. The family had already eaten, but his mother had kept his food warm on the back of the stove. Elmer came hobbling in while he was washing the dishes.

"I bet I know where you went," he said. "Ma told me the police were here. Did you catch him?"

Mark shook his head wearily. "I've got a hunch it won't be easy," he answered. "This man isn't just tough—he's clever, too."

Chapter 11

The weather stayed clear until Thanksgiving, and it was cold enough to keep the snow in fair shape. A few skiers came to the slope Thanksgiving Day and seemed to have a good time. On Friday morning Mark decided he had better prepare for the weekend. He got the oilstove, counter, and benches installed. There had been no time to build real food cupboards, but he nailed shelves in a couple of packing boxes and put them behind the counter. Then he went to Bonham's store to lay in supplies. As usual, Buck had been glad to lend him the pickup truck.

Mark had no way of telling in advance how many people he would have to feed. Later on he would be able to judge, but this time he had to take a chance. He bought six dozen frankfurters and an equal number of hot-dog rolls. To these he added a big jar of mustard, six loaves of sandwich bread, and several pounds of sliced ham. Then he thought about drinks. Two pounds of coffee were added to the load in the truck, and a couple of cases of cola drinks and pop followed. Finally he purchased a gross of paper cups and another of paper plates.

On the way home two cars full of high-school students passed him and waved. He could see that all of them had their skis. And by the time he reached the little slab-covered building at the foot of the slope, there were cars and station wagons lined up along the road for hundreds of yards. He drove on past them to the head of the line and prepared to unload. But before he could carry anything in, a state police officer hailed him.

"This your property?" the patrolman asked. "Well, these cars are blockin' the highway. You'll have to make a place for 'em to park."

With consternation Mark looked at the high snowbanks thrown up by the plow. It would take him hours just to dig through them. Moose Martin came along as he stood there.

"What's the matter?" he asked. "That cop givin' you a hard time?"

Mark told him the bad news. "If you'll give me a hand with this stuff in the truck," he said, "I'll go get my mother to come an' run the stand, an' I'll bring down a snow shovel."

Twenty minutes later he returned. Mrs. Wilkins was delighted to play short-order cook and waitress for a while. She liked young people, and Mark knew she would enjoy having a crowd of them around. Looking up at the slope, he estimated there were nearly a hundred skiers in action. He wondered if that many would come when he started charging admission.

Then he set to work. The snow was packed and heavy and the digging went slowly, but by eleven o'clock he had cut a breach wide enough for two cars through the bank. Beyond it lay an acre of fairly level ground, but the snow covered it so deeply that he knew very few cars could get through it.

He was about ready to give up, but at that moment Buck Evans appeared, carrying his skis.

"You look as if you'd lost your last friend!" he called. "What's the shovel for?"

Sadly Mark explained his predicament.

"Hold everything!" said Buck. "We'll keep you out o' jail."

He hurried off in the direction of his own place, and soon Mark heard the throaty rumble of a diesel engine. Then he saw the husky little Cat coming up the highway, its bulldozer blade attached. Buck swung in through the gap Mark had dug and lowered the blade. The snow rolled back to one side as the tractor chugged ahead. Within an hour an ample parking space had been cleared.

Mark located the owners of the various cars and persuaded them to drive in, off the road. Then he went to the lodge and looked inside. The single room was packed with laughing, chattering young people. From behind the counter his mother beamed.

"You'd better go get some more supplies," she told him. "The cokes are all gone, and there are only about a dozen hot dogs left. If this weather holds, we'll have an even bigger day tomorrow, I expect."

Once more Mark made the trip to the village and bought additional things to eat and drink. It was two o'clock before he had a chance to go up on the slope himself. He knew most of the boys and girls who were skiing, but there were also a few strangers—college men and city people. Some of the latter group, he discovered, had pulled away his brush barriers and were trying to use the upper part of the trail.

Angrily he went over to warn them. But as soon as he reached the sharp bend at the end of the ledge, he saw they had already punished themselves. One young man was sitting in the snow with a broken ski and a twisted ankle. Another lay wrapped around a tree.

For a moment Mark was scared. The figure seemed to lie very still. Then, as Mark approached, he saw it move. Dizzily the skier rolled over and tried to sit up, but the effort was too great. He groaned and fell back.

"Wha—what happened?" he gasped.

"Stay where you are and don't move," said Mark. "I'd say you had a couple o' cracked ribs. Are your legs all right?"

Gingerly the man bent first one knee and then the other.

"Good," Mark told him. "Just hold still and I'll get you to a doctor."

He unfastened the injured man's skis and strapped them side by side to form a narrow toboggan. Then he helped the patient lie down on the contraption. Before starting to tow him down the hill, he went back for a look at the other skier. He was a big, ruddy-faced collegian, and he scowled at Mark.

"That's a heck of a turn!" he complained. "Wonder I didn't break my neck!"

"Why do you suppose I had it blocked off?" Mark asked, controlling his temper. "I did it to keep folks like you from hurting yourselves. Can you walk? O.K., then—give me a hand with your friend, here."

Along the side of the trail, where people had been climbing all day, the snow was packed enough so that the man on foot didn't sink in too far. They hauled the other accident victim down to the pickup truck and lifted him carefully into the rear. Half an hour later he had been examined by a doctor in Crow Ridge. As Mark had guessed, two ribs had been broken when he hit the tree. The other skier loaded his injured friend into their car and drove off toward Philadelphia without so much as a word of thanks.

Tired and worried, Mark returned to the slope. He was getting an early initiation into some of the troubles of operating a ski run. Not that he could be blamed for what had happened. But he didn't want his hill to get a reputation for danger. Again he climbed to the top and replanted the brush barriers. Then, at last, he had a chance to schuss the trail. There was no question about it —the slope was every bit as good as he had hoped.

With the sun dropping low behind the mountain, many of the skiers were starting to leave. A few had the grace to thank Mark for letting them come. He told them he was glad they liked it and hoped they'd come back when he started charging admission next day.

Mrs. Wilkins was ready to go home and get supper. She admitted her feet were tired, but she was jubilant.

"Took in close to twenty-five dollars," she said. "I figure that's about fifteen dollars net profit. If you've got a padlock for the door, I reckon we can leave the food here. Even the pop ought to be all right. It shouldn't get below freezing inside the lodge before morning."

* * *

That night Mark knocked together a signboard three feet square and painted it yellow, so that it would show up against the snow. On the quick-drying enamel he lettered the words, "BLUEBERRY MOUNTAIN SLOPE —SKI ALL DAY—ONLY 50¢." And underneath in small letters he painted, "Mark Wilkins, Prop."

Mark turned in at the same time as the younger ones. He was tired, and he knew tomorrow would be a big day.

An inch or two of fresh snow had fallen when he rose at six, but the stars were bright in the sky and the clouds had blown clear. The temperature on the thermometer by the kitchen door stood at six above zero. It should be a perfect Saturday for skiing.

By eight o'clock he was ready to start for the slope. Elmer was whittling out another ski to take the place of the broken one, but his ankle still kept him at home. So Mark took Emily along to help at the counter, and the youngster was proud as a peacock.

The first job was to post his sign. He drove the stake

deep into the snow at the corner of the lodge, where nobody who passed could fail to see it. Then he got the stove lighted and put a big coffeepot on to boil. One thing he had remembered to do the day before was get some change. Now there was a cigar box under the counter with plenty of half dollars and smaller coins.

Emily busied herself cutting small squares of red cardboard, which would serve as tickets. On each one she wrote the date in indelible pencil. It was all her own idea, for Mark had forgotten that tickets would be needed.

Inside of the next half hour cars began to arrive, and Mark went out to steer them into the parking area. A few of the skiers looked dismayed when they saw the sign, but Mark explained that yesterday had been the only free day.

"I promised my friends," he told them with a grin, "that the first day of good snow everybody could ski for nothing. From now on I'll have to charge. The cabin's got to be paid for and the work I did on the trail. Besides, there are taxes. After all, four bits isn't much for a whole day's skiing."

Two or three pulled out, disgruntled, and said they would go somewhere else. But most of them took the news cheerfully. By the middle of the morning Emily had sold more than fifty tickets, to say nothing of coffee and a lot of her mother's doughnuts. Leaving her in charge for a few minutes, Mark climbed the trail to make sure his brush barricade was still in place. A young couple from Philadelphia were making the ascent at the same time.

"This is a lovely slope," said the girl, "but you really ought to have a ski tow. I've taken two runs, and I'm all worn out."

Mark nodded sympathetically. "I'm sort of starting on a shoestring," he told her, "and a tow is more than I can swing this winter. We'll see how things go. If the slope pays off, maybe I can afford some kind of tow next year."

The man laughed. "Don't worry too much about it," he said. "I ski for exercise, and the climbing's half the fun."

At noon Mark was back at the lodge, helping grill frankfurters and serve pop. He looked up from the stove and saw Jean Langley's laughing face. She was buying tickets for herself, another girl, and two young men. Jean waved to him gaily and they went out.

"She's nice," said Emily. "I remember when she came to our house and I liked her."

Mark didn't reply. He held out a hot dog to a hungry customer and asked if mustard was wanted. An hour later the rush of luncheon business was about over.

"You getting tired?" he asked his sister. "I'll get Mother to come down if you are."

"No," said Emily, "I love it. But we're going to need some more groceries, an' the store won't be open Sunday. You'd better go down there right now."

Mark walked to Buck's house and asked if he could borrow the truck again. "Maybe I ought to be paying you rent," he told his brother-in-law. "Anyhow I'll fill it up with gas while I'm in the village."

Buck grinned. "You can do that if you want," he said, "but I'm as anxious as you are to see the slope be a success. Who's minding the store? Emily?"

Bess heard them talking and immediately volunteered to go and help. "Emily's a smart child," she said, "but she's really too young for all that responsibility."

When he came back from Crow Ridge, Mark found the two girls in full control of the situation. He unloaded his supplies and put on his skis. It was high time, he told himself, to go up and see how things were on the trail. He had climbed a little over half the slope when he saw Jean flashing down. She was far ahead of her companions and taking the hill with expert speed. Mark cut in behind her, shot out over the bump, and landed close on the girl's heels. He hoped for a word with her before her friends arrived.

Smiling, she gave him both her hands. "Aren't you proud, Mark?" she asked. "Everybody likes your slope. The only thing I miss is that top part, with the turns."

Mark told her about yesterday's mishaps. "You wouldn't have any trouble making it," he said, "but some o' these snow-bunnies were bound to get hurt. I'll have to cut back the trees on that bend before next weekend."

"You were lucky to get a big snow so early," said Jean. "Let's hope it's a sign we'll have a white winter. If we do, I expect I'll be coming up to see you often."

"That's good news," Mark answered. "Maybe I'll have things better organized an' I can do some skiing with you."

Then her friends approached, and when he had been introduced to them, he left to go back to the lodge.

Chapter 12

When the Thanksgiving weekend was over, Mark totaled up income and expenses. From the sale of tickets, food, and soft drinks they had taken in $148.50. But they had paid out $51.20 for groceries and oil. The net profit came to $97.30, though it didn't take into account family labor, the cost of the doughnuts Mrs. Wilkins had made, or gas for the truck. On the whole Mark felt he had a right to be pretty well pleased.

As December came in, the weather grew warmer. Each day the snow shrank on the southern slopes, and rivers of water ran down every ditch and gully. Unless the thaw ended and a new storm came, Mark knew there would be no skiing the following weekend, so he devoted all his energies to school and basketball.

There had been only two seniors on the previous year's squad, and all five of the regular starters were still on hand. Coach Winton knew he was sitting pretty. His only worry was overconfidence, and when the team barely nosed out Bear Creek, he called them on the carpet.

"I guess you thought you were pretty good," he told them. "Didn't have to put out much effort against a weak outfit. Well, with a little luck Bear Creek would have pinned your ears back. Just remember that from now on."

They knew it was true, and the words sank in. That week they sharpened up their shooting. The floor play improved, too, and an ambitious second team made the varsity players hustle. Some of the sophomores and juniors had shot up like weeds since the previous year. Moose Martin's young brother Greg, who had been just an awkward kid, suddenly discovered how to handle his arms and legs and developed into a pretty good basketball player. And as soon as Elmer recovered from his sprained ankle, he began to show the same kind of speed and dribbling ability that Mark had.

The squad went down to Mt. Pocono for the second game. Off to a fast start, they took a 14-4 lead in the first five minutes, and after the other coach had called time out, Winton sent in some new men from the bench. Greg Martin took Moose's place at center and Elmer Wilkins went in at guard for Chuck Wagner.

It was the first time Mark had teamed up with his brother in the backcourt in a real game. Mt. Pocono came up the floor in a pressing defense, but Elmer took Mark's base-line pass neatly, head-faked his opponent, and dribbled across the center line like lightning. He passed back to Mark and cut for the corner, unguarded. Instead of passing in to the pivot man, Mark threw a long, hard one to his brother. Elmer jumped high to catch the ball, bounced it once, and fired from fifteen feet out—a beautiful arching shot that cut the cords. Mark felt prouder than if he had scored himself.

From that point on there was no question which was the better team. Coach Winton continued to use his substitutes freely, and by the end of the game five players had shot in double figures—two of them second-stringers. The final score was a one-sided 68-36. With real bench strength it looked as if Crow Ridge was due for another winning season.

There was only one more game before the Christmas holidays, and they won it handily. The big ones would come later, in January and February. Meanwhile, the weather turned colder once more and there was a promise of snow.

Mark and Elmer went up to the head of the bare ski slope one Saturday, carrying their axes. After a careful survey of the land Mark marked out the area he wanted cut for widening the curve. It took in a good, wide sweep, mostly above the ledge and out to the side. Then they went to work.

There were twenty or thirty trees to be felled. A few were of good size, but the bulk of the job was cutting saplings and clearing brush. By the end of the day they had stacked up nearly three cords of good firewood for seasoning, and the space for the bend in the trail was practically doubled.

"There," said Mark, leaning on his ax, "Anybody that can't make that turn has got no business trying to ski."

Elmer grinned. "Gee!" he said. "It looks so good I can hardly wait. What do you think o' those clouds?"

The sun had gone behind a gray bank in the northwest, and the wind blew shiveringly.

"I'm not the greatest weather prophet on the mountain," Mark said with a laugh, "but I'd say we might get a few flurries before morning."

It turned out his estimate was conservative. By the time they went to bed, it had started to snow. Waking some time after midnight, Mark heard the soft brush of it on the roof through the wailing of the wind. He grinned comfortably, turned over, and went to sleep again.

This was no blizzard, like the first one. Only about eight inches fell, and the sun came out by the middle of the next morning. Cars with chains or snow tires were able to negotiate the highway without much difficulty, and Buck Evans took the whole Wilkins family to church, packed in like sardines. As soon as they got home, Mark and Elmer changed their clothes and hurried to the slope.

There had been some drifting, but the trail was well covered and reasonably smooth. They took it from the top. The newly widened bend proved easy, and though Mark regretted having to spoil its sportiness, he knew it was a lot safer for ordinary skiers. He schussed on down, sailed over the bump, and landed jarringly in the shallow snow. The slope wouldn't be much fun until it had another six inches or so to cushion it.

Mark went to the sign that had fallen down when the earlier snow had melted. There was no point, he decided, in setting it up now. He didn't want to disappoint people by letting them ski until conditions were right. So he turned it around, lettered the words "NO SKIING TODAY" on the back, and stood it against the corner of the cabin.

Elmer, who had missed the big weekend, was sorry to see the sign. But he had to agree that the skiing wasn't too good.

"I'd better check up on the grub we left in here," said Mark, unlocking the lodge door. They went inside and looked in the cupboards. There was only a little food there—some bottles of pop, two loaves of stale sandwich bread, and half a dozen tired-looking frankfurters that didn't smell quite right.

"Guess it got too warm," Mark commented, wrinkling his nose. "I'll stock up again when we get some better snow. We can take this stuff home for the chickens."

He went to the corner where the big five-gallon kerosene can stood. "That's funny," he said as he lifted it. "I'd have sworn this was more'n half full. It feels empty now."

"You reckon somebody broke in?" asked Elmer. "That padlock looks kind o' flimsy."

Mark shook his head. "It worked all right when I unlocked it."

Slowly he looked around the interior and his eye lit on one of the windows. "Hey!" he said. "It's been jimmied. See those marks?"

"Golly! Who'd do a thing like that?" said Elmer. "Must ha' been a stranger. Not any o' the neighbors, that's sure."

Mark was thinking. "The last time we had robberies around here," he mused, "was way back when Mort Tuttle's gang was on the loose. I figure this must ha' been done in the last day or two, after the food spoiled. Any thief that took oil would probably want the bread an' franks, too."

He wedged the window with a piece of wood, locked the door again, and went down to the Evanses' to use the telephone. When he called the state police barracks, he was told Sergeant Green was out on patrol. But he gave the man at the desk an account of what had happened.

"Not much of a burglary," said the officer, "but I agree it's not the sort o' thing we like around this part o' the country. I'll tell the sergeant, and I expect he'll be 'round to see you."

Buck had been standing by while Mark made his call. "You know," he said, "this sure ties in with what I said last winter. Whoever stole that oil didn't want to be seen around a store. He's probably hiding out somewhere in the woods, an' I reckon he's got a lantern—maybe even an oil cookstove. It all sounds like the same guy that took a shot at you. We know he's killing deer and he's a pretty desperate character. If his name isn't Mort Tuttle, I'm going to be surprised."

Sergeant Green was waiting for Mark when he came out of school on Monday. He asked to hear the details again and rubbed his chin thoughtfully as he listened. Then he said almost the same thing Buck had.

"This fellow wasn't looking for cash or jewelry," he commented, "though I expect he'd have taken them if they'd been handy. What he wanted was kerosene, an' all he stole was about seventy-five cents' worth. He must be keeping out of sight—not wanting anybody to spot him buying things. I don't believe it was kids. You say there were some bottled drinks that weren't touched, an' that would be the first thing they'd go for. I'm beginning to think it may be that poacher we chased."

"Have any of your men seen him?" Mark asked.

"No, but we've had a couple of other leads since I talked to you. One thing, there was a jeep panel truck stolen over in Jersey last year and never recovered. The description fits the one we think he drives. And then a week ago the game warden got a tip that a big roadhouse down near Easton was having a venison banquet for a sportsmen's club. The man that told him had seen a jeep panel job backed up to the kitchen door, and he thought they were unloading deer. Jones followed up on it, but the proprietors claimed they got their venison from a meat wholesaler in New York—never had dealings with any jeep owner. We're pretty sure they're lying, but it's tough to prove."

Mark felt frustrated. He drove with the sergeant as far as the ski cabin, showed him the marks of the jimmy on the window, and let him examine the inside. As he expected, the policeman found no clues. The theft had evidently taken place before the last snow, and any tracks the burglar might have left were well covered now. He said good-by to Sergeant Green and went on home.

Elmer was studying a mail-order catalog when Mark came in. He had the big book open on his knees and was jotting down figures on a piece of paper.

"Know what?" said the younger boy. "I bet we could build a ski tow for less'n fifteen hundred dollars!"

Mark laughed. "That's right," he said. "We could buy

a pretty nice used car, too. Or a motorboat. If we had the fifteen hundred, that is."

"Yeah," replied Elmer, not in the least perturbed. "But a ski tow would make money—even a homemade rope tow like I was thinking about."

"How do you figure the cost?" asked Mark, beginning to be interested.

"Well," the boy explained, "we could put up the poles an' crossarms ourselves—for just what our time's worth. Then we'd have to have five thousand feet o' one-inch rope. That would go up about half a mile an' back. At sixteen cents a foot, that's eight hundred bucks. The iron work—pulleys an' such—would come to another seventy-five dollars. Then, o' course, we'd have to get some kind of an engine an' build a shed over it. I'm pretty sure we could get that for under five hundred."

Mark took the paper with Elmer's notes on it. After

some study he nodded. "Looks all right," he said. "I think you'd have to go higher for pulleys, though. Ought to allow at least a hundred bucks. An' there are always expenses you aren't looking for. We'd better put down another hundred an' call it 'miscellaneous.' Now, let's see—that adds up to an even thousand. I don't know how much horsepower it would take, but I bet I can get a good used engine for less than you guessed. Looks as if you're right—fifteen hundred dollars ought to cover it."

He thought about the plan after he went to bed. It would have to be the simplest kind of tow—no chairs, of course. The skiers would just hold on to hand ropes and be pulled up the slope. They couldn't charge much for the service either. It would probably have to be included in the over-all price of a ticket. Perhaps a dollar for a day's skiing would be satisfactory to the customers. Then, sooner or later, the government would come around and tell him he had to charge and pay 10 per cent for an amusement tax. At least, that's what it was at the movies, and he supposed it applied to a ski run, too.

He could worry about that when the time came. A much bigger problem now was where to raise fifteen hundred dollars. They would have to wait till spring to set the poles, when the ground was soft enough for digging. So for the present there was nothing that could be done about it anyhow. At last, still wrestling with the figures, he drifted off to sleep.

All week long Mark listened hopefully to the weather forecasts on the radio. There was a big high over the eastern states, holding back a cold front that had brought heavy snow to Minnesota, Wisconsin, and Michigan. Finally, on Thursday night, the weatherman promised clouds and probable snow flurries for the next day.

It started to snow Friday morning, but the flakes fell for only an hour or two. Under a leaden sky Mark came home from school. The wind had shifted to the northeast now, and the temperature had dropped. By the time he had finished the chores and was coming in from the barn, the snow had begun once more.

On Saturday he had to take only one look out the window to know his hopes had been fulfilled. The clouds were beginning to break away, but nearly a foot of fresh snow lay on the ground!

Unceremoniously he pulled Elmer out of bed. "Come on, kid," he told him. "Plenty o' good skiing today. You'd better dig some paths while I milk."

The instant breakfast was over, Mark headed for Buck's to borrow the truck. The snow tires enabled him to get through to the village. Then, with a fresh load of groceries, he hurried back to the ski lodge. By the time the plows came through, he had restocked the food cupboards, put the coffeepot on, and replaced the sign that announced the slope was open. He was all set for what he hoped would be another good weekend.

Chapter 13

Cars began to arrive early. Once more Mark had to get Buck's tractor to clear the parking lot, for with the new snow it was covered too deeply for easy access. Soon Elmer came down, followed by Emily. They did a brisk business despite the fact that nearly all the skiers so far were local people.

Mark had time during the day for two or three runs down the slope. The surface was almost perfect, and the new bend around the ledge made a fine addition to the trail. All the better skiers were using it and praising it. The less experienced ones were content to start lower down.

At the end of the day there were still enough frankfurters and rolls for the expected Sunday crowd. Mark put them in big paper bags for Elmer and Emily to carry home. He left several cases of pop in the cabin, along with the oil can. But the money was a different matter. From the farm he had brought a handy-sized cotton salt bag that held the bills and coins nicely. This he stuffed in the pocket of his Mackinaw before locking up, then hurried after his brother and sister.

"You know something?" said Elmer when he overtook them. "Four different people today asked why we didn't sell skis an' poles an' ski boots. I bet we could make quite a lot o' money on 'em if we did."

"Sure," Mark replied, taking Emily's bundle of food. "I'd thought about it, too. It would take a pretty big investment at the start, an' we'd have to stock a good many sizes. But once we've got a going concern here, I reckon we might try it."

Starting a ski slope, as he had already discovered, was fairly simple. It was the following steps, like a tow and a decent inventory of ski goods, that would pile up the costs. Thinking it over, he resolved that he wouldn't be stampeded into expanding too fast. What they had now was more than enough to pay the taxes and add a little extra income.

Sunday came in cold and clear. Mark went down early to get the lodge ready, but his mother was firm in insisting that the rest of the family should go to church. So until noon Mark did everything himself. The crowd that morning was different, largely made up of college students and people from downstate. They all seemed to want coffee and sandwiches at once, and Mark was kept on the jump waiting on them. About eleven-thirty, when the first rush was over and the noon lunches hadn't yet started, a stranger came down off the slope, stood his skis in the snow, and entered the cabin. He was a pleasant-faced man of thirty or thirty-five, dressed in the best of ski clothes. He wandered over to the counter and leaned his elbows on its top.

"Coffee?" asked Mark. "Hot dog? Homemade doughnuts?"

The man grinned amiably. "Coffee," he said, "and a couple of doughnuts. Do you own this place?"

"My family does. I cleared the trail and built the lodge. I guess you come from the city?"

The stranger sipped his coffee. "That's right," he said. "Philadelphia. My name's Clyde Roebuck, and I do a sports broadcast on radio every night."

"Gee!" Mark gasped. "I thought there was something about your voice—why, I listen to you a lot! Especially when you talk about snow conditions in the different ski areas."

"I like to ski," said Roebuck with a nod. "Sunday's about the only chance I get, so it's nice to find a good slope so near. I drove up in only a bit over two hours. You've just opened this winter, haven't you?"

"Thanksgiving weekend," Mark replied. "How'd you like the trail?"

"Fine! Coming down I wouldn't mind having it a bit longer, but climbing up, it's plenty long. First-rate exercise, though."

Mark laughed. "A tow's something that'll have to come later," he said. "This way we get folks who really love to ski."

"I bet you get a few who really love good doughnuts, too. Who made these?"

"My mother. She's the best cook on the mountain, bar none."

"I'd like to meet her," said the sportscaster. "If I don't, be sure to give her my compliments. Your name's Mark Wilkins, isn't it? Any relation to Elmer Wilkins, the author?"

"Yes," said Mark. "He was my dad."

"I've read the book," Roebuck replied. "Liked it, too. Well, keep listening. I'll be on the air again tomorrow night, you know. So long for now. I'm going up for another schuss."

When he had left, Mark wiped the counter top, absorbed in thought. Clyde Roebuck was one of the most popular radio commentators in the East. If he gave a plug to the Blueberry Mountain slope—but that was more than the boy dared to hope.

Soon the family returned from church, and he had help with the lunchtime crowd. By one-thirty they had run out of supplies, and he had to turn down a few hungry latecomers. Knowing how much to buy, it seemed, was another headache for operators of ski slopes.

As the sun dropped behind the mountain, cars began to pull out of the parking space. A few people kept on skiing until the afterglow turned to dusk. Mark sent Elmer and Emily home while he waited for the last enthusiasts to rack their skis and depart. Then he counted the total take for the two days and put it in the salt sack. To his surprise there was just over $200, about half of it in silver.

Darkness had fallen when he locked the cabin and started up the road toward home. The bag was too bulky for his pocket, so he tied it tightly and carried it swinging from his hand. A half moon hung in the southern sky, giving him enough light to see where he was going. He stayed on the left side of the plowed-out highway, facing traffic, though for the first three hundred yards he saw no cars.

Fairly close to his own road now, he started to cut over to the right. Suddenly he heard the throb of an engine close behind him. There were no lights. But at that instant the engine roared louder, and the vehicle charged ahead as if trying to run him down. Mark dodged back again to his left, slipped on the icy roadway, and fell into the banked snow at the side.

"Stay where y'are!" a hoarse voice snarled. "Put up yer hands or I'll shoot!"

Mark saw the dark shape of a jeep panel truck jerking to a stop almost on top of him. Out of it jumped a stocky figure with a rifle. Mark acted on instinct. He threw the sack of money as far as he could into the brush. Then, in the same motion, he rolled over, regained his feet, and ducked around the rear of the truck. Not even waiting to see if the man was following, he sprinted across the road and dove for cover in a hemlock thicket.

He couldn't stay there. Already he could hear the man's feet pounding after him. In desperation he crawled on his belly downhill to the right, trying to move silently in the brush. There were thrashing sounds from the spot where he had gone in. Breathless, he wriggled on a few yards till he was in the densest part of the thicket. Then he lay as still as a rabbit in its form.

For a minute that seemed like an hour, the driver of the jeep poked and prodded among the hemlocks, cursing all the while under his breath. Then he turned away, hurrying back across the road. He climbed up into the brush on that side and began another search. This time, Mark realized, he was hunting for the bag of money. And there was nothing the boy could do about it but wait silently and hope.

Perhaps, he thought, a car would come along and stop to see what was wrong with the jeep. Or perhaps the white salt bag would be hard to see against the snow, and the man would give up his search. But both wishes were in vain. After two or three minutes he heard a grunt of satisfaction, and the robber came scrambling back to the road holding the sack of money in one fist, the rifle in the other.

Mark could see him more plainly as he went toward the panel truck. The lower part of his face was covered by a dark, bushy beard, and he had on a shapeless jacket that looked gray in the moonlight. He cast one look toward the brush where Mark lay hidden, then climbed into the jeep and started the engine. The truck lights came on as he drove swiftly off up the highway.

As soon as he was gone, Mark came out of the thicket and went down to the Evans farm at a run. He was so short of breath when he got there that he could only gasp out a word or two to Buck. Then he went to the wall telephone and called the police barracks.

Sergeant Green's voice answered. He heard Mark's account of what had happened with deep concern, but said he couldn't leave the desk for a while.

"Trooper Molloy's out your way somewhere," he told the boy. "Probably not too far off. I'll give him a call on the car radio. Just sit tight and he'll pick you up at the Evans place."

Molloy arrived fifteen minutes later. He was the same young patrolman who had warned Mark that he had to make a parking place for cars. Obviously he was inexperienced, but he took his job seriously. First of all, he got out a notebook and laboriously wrote down all the details Mark could remember. Then, with a stern look, he drew his revolver and made sure it was loaded.

"Accordin' to your statement, the suspect is armed an' may be dangerous," said Molloy. "If you'll come with me, we'll proceed to the scene o' the crime."

Over the trooper's shoulder Buck winked at Mark. He, too, had noticed how much the remark sounded like a police report.

The patrolman unbent a little after they were in the car. "Darn shame," he said, "just as you were getting your ski slope well started."

He drove slowly up the highway till they came to the spot where Mark had nearly been run down.

"Right there," said the boy. "You can see the skid marks where he jammed on the brakes after I ducked. Right up yonder's where I tossed the sack of money, an' those deep footprints in the snow are where he climbed up to hunt for it."

"How much did you say was in the sack?" asked Molloy.

"The whole two days' take from the skiing. I'd counted it once, in the cabin, an' it came out to two hundred an' three dollars. But you know how it is, trying to count a whole mess o' halves an' quarters an' dimes. I might have been a little off, but not more'n a dollar."

"You had a light in the cabin?" asked the trooper. "A lantern?"

"That's right. I suppose anybody looking in the window could have seen all that dough spread out on the counter. Maybe he'd parked the jeep back a way an' sneaked up to watch me."

Molloy nodded. "Sounds like it," he said. "We'll take a look for tracks when we go back. Now—after he found the money—he started the truck an' went on up this way?"

"Yes. He'd switched on his lights by then. The last I saw was the taillight going over that rise."

The police car drove on up the highway for several miles and turned right on the Bear Creek road, which had also been plowed out.

"See if you can spot that little woods trail," said the trooper. "The place you an' the sergeant found the jeep tracks."

Mark watched the right-hand side as they moved slowly northward. They passed the farmhouse where Green had used the phone, and he knew the hidden woods road was only a short distance farther.

"Take it easy," he warned Molloy. "We're getting close now. See where those tracks pull out?"

The trooper slowed the car to a walking pace, turned on his spotlight, and aimed it to the right. There was no doubt about it. Freshly made tire tracks led up the narrow trail into the woods. Cautiously, Molloy swung into the same ruts, but at once they were in trouble. The snow, more than a foot deep, was too much for the low-slung car. The rear wheels spun, the engine raced, then faltered and stalled.

"Can't follow him in there," the patrolman growled. "He's got more clearance an' four-wheel drive. Snow don't bother him like it does us."

He started the engine again, eased into reverse, and succeeded in backing out. Then he put on the parking brake and picked up the hand microphone that hung on the dash.

"Car Eighteen," he said, "calling Sergeant Green."

There was a brief wait before the sergeant came on. Then Mark heard him answer, his voice coming from the speaker under the dash.

"Green here," he said. "Go ahead, Eighteen."

Molloy explained the situation. "Only way to go in after him is afoot," he said. "Unless you can send up a four-wheel drive truck. Looks like the suspect made it without any trouble."

"Afraid we're just out o' four-wheel drives," the sergeant replied with a chuckle. "But at least he's bottled up in there. I'll send another car to relieve you, and when it gets there, you can take Wilkins on home."

They sat in the car for twenty minutes, talking in low voices. Once, years before, Mark had watched at the mouth of a foxhole all one afternoon. He found later that the fox had left by a back exit and was long gone. Now he wondered if this vigil would end the same way. At last they saw lights approaching, and a state police car pulled up. Molloy got out to brief the other patrolman, then drove Mark back to the ski lodge.

The snow around the cabin was pretty well packed by skis, but there was one place, at the end where the stove and counter stood, where somebody had waded close to the window. The footprints were made by heavy rubber-soled boots, quite different from ski boots.

"This is where he was, all right," said Mark. "He could see everything I did as plain as day through the window here."

"Well," Molloy replied, fishing out his notebook, "I'll make a report on it. Don't worry—we'll catch him sooner or later, an' I expect you'll get your money back."

It was seven-thirty when Mark finally reached home, and supper was long since eaten. He hurried out to milk while his mother warmed up some food for him. It wasn't until he was at the table that he had a chance to tell the family what had happened.

"Two hundred an' three dollars!" he groaned. "All we collected in two good days! It's enough to make a guy turn sour on the world."

Mrs. Wilkins tried to comfort him. "We've still got enough to last out the week," she said. "And with the state troopers on the job, maybe the thief'll be caught. Anyhow, let's not give up hope yet."

Tossing in bed that night, Mark thought again about the fox. The longer he lay awake, the surer he became that the bearded man would find a way to elude the police. If he was going to recover his money, he decided, it was up to him to do something himself.

Chapter 14

The sky was cloudy Monday morning. The temperature, Mark saw, had risen a little and stood close to the freezing line. He thought it might rain before the day was over.

Waiting till his mother had left the kitchen to rouse the others, he took his rifle and snowshoes outside and hid them under the porch. Then he did the chores, ate breakfast with his brothers and sisters, and put on his Mackinaw and cap. It was time to go down to the school bus. As they left the house, he let the smaller ones run on ahead and motioned to Elmer to wait.

"I won't be going to school today," he said in a low voice. "Tell my room teacher I'm sick. I really am, too—sick about losing all that money. Now go on down as if nothing was happening."

"Gee!" whispered Elmer, his eyes big as saucers. "You going out with the cops again?"

Mark shook his head. "I'm just skipping school, an' that's all I can tell you."

When Elmer had left, he went to the hiding place under the porch and took out the things he had left there. A moment later, with his snowshoes on, he was moving through the woods toward the cutover land. Near the edge of the brush he waited till the bus was out of sight, then crossed the ski slope, and went to the Evans place. Buck was just coming in from the barn.

"Hi!" the young farmer called. "What's up? No school today?"

"Not for me, anyhow," Mark answered with a grin. "I wonder if you'd be too busy to do a little hunting with me—back over the mountain. I'm not after deer."

Buck listened to him soberly as he outlined his plan. "I don't know," he answered at last. "Running quite a risk, aren't you? Why not let the police handle it?"

"Their idea," said Mark, "is just to watch that woods trail an' catch him when he comes out. But I figure he's too smart. He'll know they're there. Either he's got a back trail where he can drive the jeep, or he can leave it where it is an' go out on snowshoes. The longer we give him, the less chance I've got of finding my money."

Buck still looked doubtful, but he finally agreed to come along. "Just one thing," he said. "I'm going to tell Bess that if we aren't back here by two o'clock, she's to call Sergeant Green."

Ten minutes later they were on their way up the shoulder of the mountain. Mark knew exactly where he was going, and after an hour or more of steady progress they neared the rocky ridge beyond the swamp. There they moved with greater caution. As they crept through the undergrowth, a startled doe jumped out just ahead of them and went bounding away through the snow.

"Well," Mark whispered, "he's not very close by or he'd have taken a shot at the deer. I reckon it's safe to climb the ridge."

They went up to the crest, keeping in the shelter of rocks and trees. A careful scrutiny showed nobody on the other side. Down the hill they scrambled over the ledges and through the brush, till they came to the edge of the ravine.

"He sure didn't drive out this way," Buck whispered. "Look down there. It's solid with rhododendron. Probably a stream there in the bottom."

Mark nodded. "He could have made it afoot, though. I'm going down an' see. You stay up here an' cover me."

Before Buck could voice an objection, Mark was moving down the precipitous slope, catching at rocks and trees to keep from falling. The ravine was close to a hundred feet deep, and in many places its sides went up like the walls of a house. As he neared the bottom, he was in half-darkness, for even if the sun had been shining, very little light could penetrate that far. Then he plunged into the jungle of rhododendron. The thick stems writhed like snakes around him, caught at his snowshoes, and made progress almost impossible. It was certain that the robber had not escaped through this tangle.

Mark rested a minute, then clawed his way back to the ravine wall he had descended. Just above the thicket there was a kind of shelf running along the side. The snow on it showed no tracks, but something about the look of the ledge made him think it might have been used as a path. Perhaps deer came this way to drink when the stream wasn't frozen.

He looked upward but could see nothing of Buck. Not wanting to call out, he waited a moment, then set off along the ledge, moving down the ravine. When he had gone perhaps a hundred yards, he stopped suddenly with his heart in his mouth. There in front of him were snowshoe tracks!

They pointed in both directions; some headed toward him, others down the ravine. But all, he was sure, were made by the same man. At the spot where he first sighted them, the tracks turned suddenly and climbed the steep bank on his left. There was a narrow gap between clumps of laurel bushes, and that was where they disappeared.

Mark stood still, holding his breath and listening. Somewhere far above he heard a twig snap faintly. The sound seemed to come from the top of the ravine wall, where Buck should be. Very carefully he moved back a couple of steps. And the raucous cry of a blue jay came from ten feet away, so startlingly close that he almost dropped his rifle. Still squawking angrily, the bird flew off up the valley.

Again Mark waited. Surely if the poacher were near, he would hear the alarm and take some action. But the woods had settled to stillness once more. After a dozen heartbeats the boy backed up a few more yards. He had to find out where those tracks led, but he didn't want to follow them directly. There was too much danger of walking into an ambush.

With the greatest care he started climbing the bank. The tough stem of a laurel bush gave him a handhold, and he went upward a step at a time till he was five or six feet above the ledge. From there he had a view through the brush along the side of the ravine. The first thing he saw was a bare rock crag looming almost straight up. Then, at about the same level as his eyes, he made out some kind of break in the forbidding wall of stone. The more he studied it, the surer he became that he was looking at the entrance to a cave.

Mark wished fervently that he could signal to Buck, but that might be fatal. Instead, he inched nearer the opening in the rock, moving as silently as possible and holding his gun ready. When he was three or four yards away, he could see the snowshoe tracks again. They led straight to the shadowy gap in the cliff!

The boy's tension mounted. He could feel trickles of sweat running down his cheeks. How could he tell whether his enemy was inside the cave? Looking around him, he found a broken stick in the snow, and with his left hand he threw it at the opening. It bounced against the rock with a crackling sound. Mark braced himself and held his breath, but nothing happened.

Then, through the brush, he caught a glimpse of movement down the trail. Something was coming. A heavy figure appeared, moving along the ledge on snowshoes. He could see the rough gray jacket, the cap, and the dark, bushy beard. Swinging in the man's hand was a rifle.

Mark cocked the Winchester. Now that the time had come, he was no longer scared. He felt cool and steady. He waited till the bearded man was right below him, starting to climb the slope. Then he acted.

"Drop the gun!" he barked, his voice hard and sharp. "Drop it an' put up your hands!"

Taken completely by surprise, the man slipped and fell backward, the rifle flying out of his grasp. Before he could reach for it, Mark was standing above him, the sights leveled on his chest.

"Hold it right there," the boy ordered. "Don't make a move or I'll have to kill you. Hey—Buck!"

He yelled the last words at the top of his lungs, and an instant later the crashing of brush above told him his friend was on his way down. Surly but helpless, the whiskered robber sat where he had fallen, his beady eyes fixed on the unwavering rifle muzzle.

From twenty feet above Buck looked down. He saw what was happening, shouted a word of encouragement to Mark, and hurried over to one side of the cliff, where he could scramble down. A minute later he was on the ledge, picking up the man's rifle.

"Good going!" he panted with a grin. "What'll we do with him?"

"Just keep him covered for a bit," Mark answered. "I'd like to take a look at the cave."

He turned, climbed another step or two, and stood in the shadowy entrance. The cleft in the rock was little more than a yard wide, and he had to stoop to enter. Once inside, he struck a match and looked around. The cave

was bigger than he expected—an irregular chamber a dozen feet deep and half as wide. He saw a pile of rumpled, dirty blankets in a corner, a sooty lantern, and an oilcan. On a ledge there was a side of bacon and half a loaf of bread. The rock floor showed traces of a cooking fire, with a skillet and a battered coffeepot still sitting in the ashes.

The match in his hand went out, but his eyes were better adjusted to the dim light now. He went over to the heap of bedding and stirred it with his rifle butt. There came a clinking noise from under the blankets. Quickly, he pulled the blankets aside and saw what he had been looking for. There it was—the salt bag, still fat and heavy. He picked it up and went back into the open air. The pair below hadn't moved an inch, but he could hear Buck's voice talking quietly.

"Beard or no beard, I'd know you," the young farmer was saying. "You've got the same shifty eyes you always had. Soon as we turn you over to the police, they'll fingerprint you an' prove it."

Mark came down to the path, holding the white bag triumphantly. "Here's the money he stole," he said. "Or most of it, anyhow. I'll have to count it before I'm sure. Who is he—Mort Tuttle?"

Buck nodded without taking his eyes off the prisoner. "O.K.," he ordered. "Get on your feet, Tuttle. We'll take a walk down to the jeep."

The man stood up warily. "You got me all wrong," he whined. "My name's Thomas, an' I didn't have no place to stay, so I come up here lookin' fer a cave where I could sleep."

"Seems to me you found it mighty easy," said Mark. "Go on—get moving."

In single file they marched down the ravine. The path was well enough marked, evidently from frequent use.

After about a quarter of a mile they came to the jeep panel truck, deep in the snow.

"That yours?" asked Buck.

"Never seen it before," the man replied sullenly.

Mark laughed. "I doubt if you'll ever see it again, either," he told him. "Just keep walking."

Five minutes later they were within sight of the Bear Creek road. Buck kept the prisoner covered while Mark hurried on ahead. As he had hoped, the police were still maintaining a stake-out, and he saw Trooper Molloy sitting in a black-and-white car a hundred feet up the road.

"Hey!" the boy called, and waved his rifle. "We've got him! Got the money, too!"

The car started up and came down to the entrance of the ravine trail. Molloy stared, goggle-eyed, as Buck prodded the captive forward. They put him in the back seat, with Buck on guard beside him. Then, as they drove down the mountain, Mark told the patrolman their story.

"I knew he must have a hide-out in there," he concluded. "An' as long as Buck was willing to go with me, I figured we'd better find it before he got out the back way on snowshoes. We think he's Mort Tuttle. You can tell for sure when you take his prints."

Molloy called the barracks, and there was quite a reception committee waiting when they drove up. Sergeant Green and two other troopers hustled the prisoner out of the car and into a cell.

"He says he doesn't know anything about that jeep truck," Mark told the sergeant. "But I'd like to bet he's got the keys to it in his pocket."

Green chuckled. "That's one bet I wouldn't take," he said. "You did a good job, son. Made us look a little silly. I'd considered going in on the trail with snowshoes, but I knew he'd probably have the drop on us. Your way was better, coming in from behind. Now sit down there an' count the money. I doubt if he's had a chance to spend any."

The coins and greenbacks were all there—two hundred and three dollars, as Mark had figured. He asked Green if he had to leave it for evidence and was told, to his joy, that he could take the money away. Molloy drove them to the Evans farm in his car.

"Gosh, Buck," said Mark, "I don't know just how to thank you. I couldn't have done much without your help."

"Forget it!" His brother-in-law laughed. "I wouldn't have missed the fun for a hundred dollars! Come in for some lunch, and I'll drive you down to school. You don't want to skip a whole day."

Mark left the money with Bess for safekeeping and got to the school building in time for afternoon classes. When basketball practice was over, he came home in the bus as usual.

There was no point in trying to deceive his mother. He was sure the smaller children had told her he hadn't gone with them that morning. So he made a clean breast of it.

"All I missed was a couple o' morning classes," he said. "And I did get the two hundred dollars back. Besides, you won't have to be worried any more when the kids go up in the woods. Mort Tuttle's safe in jail."

She tried to look stern, then threw her arms around him. "I hate to admit it," she said with a laugh, "but I guess you did right. If I'd had any idea where you were, I'd have been scared every minute. All I can say now is I'm proud of you."

He did the chores, ate supper, and sat down with his books at the kitchen table. Elmer and Emily were doing their homework in the other room, with the radio going, as usual. Suddenly he heard his brother let out a whoop.

"Hey, Mark!" cried Elmer. "Clyde Roebuck's on, an' guess who he's talkin' about—us!"

Chapter 15

Mark jumped up and hurried in to listen. The friendly voice of the sports commentator was rattling on at its usual rapid-fire rate.

"One thing you'll be glad to hear," Roebuck was saying, "is that the new slope is easy to reach. Two hours and twenty minutes from City Hall. I timed it, and I wasn't exceeding the speed limit. There's no tow yet, but real skiers won't mind a little climbing. Good for the muscles and the wind, boys! Young Mr. Wilkins has built a snug little lodge where the eats are first-class. His mother makes the doughnuts—about the best I ever tasted. They're practically worth the trip, even if you're a snow-bunny! So here's a ski spot I'm happy to recommend. Don't forget the name—Blueberry Mountain Slope—four miles up from Crow Ridge."

He went on to describe ski conditions at better-known resorts, covering Pennsylvania, New York, and the big New England areas, then turned to other sports.

"Golly!" Elmer breathed. "Think of it! Our own place, on the air!"

Mark shared his excitement. "Did you hear that, Mom?" he called. "About the doughnuts? If we still have good snow next weekend, you'll have to make a double order!"

His mother had been putting the smaller ones to bed and had missed the radio plug. They had to repeat it for her, word for word, interrupting each other to add choice bits.

"Now, Mother," said Emily, starry-eyed, "you know how it feels to be famous!"

They were still congratulating themselves on what the broadcast might bring in the way of business when they heard the drumming of rain on the roof. Mark went to look at the thermometer and returned dejected. It was up to forty now, and the rain had settled to a steady downpour.

By breakfast time the next morning much of the snow was gone. There was still no sign of a letup in the rain. All they could do was hope for colder temperatures and another snow before the end of the week.

Mark had never thought much about the weather until now. Where it came from and how men could forecast its movements were a mystery to him, but he meant to find out some of the answers. He went to his science teacher one day that week. Mr. Githens was a young man, an ex-Air Force officer who had studied meteorology. He was glad to explain how weather was plotted.

From his desk drawer he got out a blank map of the United States. Then he opened the morning newspaper to the weather map and showed Mark the high- and low-pressure areas.

"Weather almost always moves from west to east," he said. "Yesterday a front of low pressure came across the Alleghenies out of the Midwest and gave us all that rain. It was followed by the high you see here, and it's cleared off a little colder. Now back up there in the Dakotas is a real cold front, moving slowly eastward. They've had plenty of snow with it, and ordinarily I'd say it should reach us in about forty-eight hours. You can't tell for sure, though. If our high-pressure area gets anchored off the coast as it sometimes does, it might hold back the cold front or push it off to the northeast. If that happens, New York and New England could have snow while it stays fair here."

He went on to show how the winds move around centers of pressure—clockwise around a high, counterclockwise around a low. "That's why we have strong south winds ahead of a low-pressure front," he said. "And as soon as it's past, the wind shifts to the north or northeast. Do you get a daily paper at home?"

"No," said Mark. "We hear the weather report on the radio, though."

"Good. Take a few of these blank maps along and chart your own from the forecast. Here's the newspaper map to show you how it's done."

From that time on, Mark made a real study of the subject. He watched the barometer in the physics lab and listened carefully to the radio weather report. Wind direction began to mean something to him, too. All that week the "Bermuda High" off the coast kept the skies clear and the temperature above normal. A southerly breeze blew steadily. It was fine weather for everybody but skiers.

As December advanced toward the holidays, Mark grew really worried. Before and after Christmas, snow would mean more than at any other time. Meanwhile, he heard unhappily that the skiing was excellent in the Adirondacks and Vermont. Each weekend thousands of people from Pennsylvania journeyed north by car, bus, train, and plane.

On the last day of school before the start of Christmas vacation, Mr. Githens stopped Mark in the hall and asked him to come to the science room. "Got something to show you," he said. "I think it's good news."

He pulled out a map, explaining that he had just talked to the weathermen at the Tri-City Airport.

"There's a deep trough of low pressure right here over Michigan," he said, pointing with his finger. "It's moving fast—pushed along by a cold air mass out of Canada. If the front keeps coming at the same speed, it ought to reach here before tomorrow night. And when it hits this damp, warm air from the south—look out for snow!"

"You figure the high won't hold this one back?" Mark asked hopefully.

"The odds are at least three-to-one it won't. Too much power behind the cold front. So if I were you, I'd lay in supplies and get ready for a blizzard."

Late that afternoon Mark drove the pickup to Bonham's store and bought a lot of groceries. The clerks laughed at him, sure the warm weather would hold, but he made his purchases and drove home. It was a pleasure to unlock the ski cabin once more. Inside, the forty-degree chill assured him that his supplies would keep, and he locked up again, returned the truck, and walked home. Overhead, there were high clouds blowing out of the northwest.

The next day there was a restless feeling in the air. Mark's skin prickled. He knew without looking at a barometer that a weather change was brewing. By three in the afternoon the sky had darkened to a dull gray, and before dusk it began to snow. The moment the first flakes drifted down, the boy's spirits rose.

"This is going to be a good one," he told Elmer as they did the chores. "I bet we'll be out digging paths by morning."

All night long the storm continued. Mark could hear the wind moaning around the eaves and the muffled hiss of the snow. It wasn't blowing as hard as in some other storms, so he knew there would be less drifting. But the cold crept through the house walls. He wasn't surprised, when he looked at the thermometer in the morning, to find the mercury right at the zero mark.

The snow was close to a foot in depth and showed no signs of letting up. Mark and Elmer dug the paths, as the older boy had prophesied. Then, with the morning work out of the way, they went inside to get warm. Mrs. Wilkins had been listening to the radio news.

"This storm's supposed to last another twelve hours," she told them. "For Philadelphia, they predict fourteen inches of snow, and more farther north. It begins to look as if you'll get some holiday business, son."

"That's not all the news," Emily put in. "Mort Tuttle's been indicted by the Grand Jury. Armed robbery and killing illegal deer. His trial comes up in February, but they're keeping him locked up because he couldn't raise the money for bail."

* * *

By Monday morning the sun was shining again, but the air stayed bitterly cold. The roads had been plowed out. Mark put on his skis and went out to try the slope. There on the mountain he found a smooth cover nearly eighteen inches deep. He climbed to the top of the trail and came zooming down on a surface that was close to perfect.

Now that the schools and colleges were out, he knew he could expect skiers any day of the week, so he went down for Buck's tractor and plowed out half an acre for parking. Before noon a few cars had driven in and Emily had sold nearly thirty tickets.

From twelve o'clock on, business at the lunch counter was brisk. It was surprising how many people asked for doughnuts and said they had heard about them on the Clyde Roebuck broadcast. Luckily, Mark's mother had made a big batch of them that morning, and Elmer brought them down piping hot in a covered bushel basket.

More and more cars arrived as the afternoon wore on.

The take for the day was less than on a good Saturday or Sunday, but Mark was well satisfied. According to his interpretation of the weather forecast, they could expect fair skies and low temperatures for the next three or four days at least.

The only complaint the skiers had was the cold. The cookstove gave some warmth at the counter end of the lodge, but the rest of the room was chilly. Mark knew he would have to buy some kind of oil heater. In the meantime, he had another idea.

He and his brother brought sleds down from the house and loaded them with wood at the top of the slope, where the curve had been widened. Much of it was pine, which didn't need seasoning to burn well. Thirty or forty feet from the cabin they built a bonfire, and from then on there was a group of young people around it most of the time.

Mark waited till dark when nearly all the skiers had left, then took the pickup truck down to Crow Ridge. At

Bonham's store he purchased more supplies. Then he asked the proprietor if he had an oil heater in stock.

"Hm," said the storekeeper, "seems like I did see one in the back room last time I took inventory. Come on; let's have a look."

Like most country stores, this one carried a little of everything. Fast-selling items, such as groceries, dry goods, drugs, and Christmas toys, were displayed in the front. Behind that there was a big, dingy room filled with tools and farm implements, tires, fertilizer, lanterns, and assorted hardware. Finally, in a dusty corner beneath a pile of rope and ax handles, Mr. Bonham uncovered an oil-stove. It was of sheet iron, not very big but in fair condition when the dust was brushed off.

"I've had it too long," the storekeeper said. "Let ye have it fer just what it cost me—nine dollars an' a half. If it don't work right, bring it back."

Mark paid him for the heater and the groceries, bought an extra can of kerosene, and went back to the lodge. Elmer and Emily were already gone, but he lighted the lantern and set up the heater in the cold end of the room. After putting in oil, he started it up. The circular flame burned clean, and after a few preliminary pops, as the metal expanded, the stove gave out a surprising amount of heat. Mark was pleased with his purchase. If it kept the customers happy, it was well worth the cost. He made sure it was safely turned off before he locked the door and went home.

He said nothing to the family about the new investment. In the morning when Emily arrived at the cabin, he already had both stoves lighted, and a pleasant warmth was beginning to fill the room. His sister stared in amazement.

"Mark!" she cried. "You got it! Now everybody'll be comfortable."

As he had expected, a bigger crowd came that day. He had little time to enjoy the slope himself, but he didn't mind as long as the patrons were having fun. One of the new arrivals was a family from Easton with two young children. There was a girl of nine or ten and a seven-year-old boy, both equipped with skis to fit their size.

"I wonder," their father asked Mark, "if you could give these kids some lessons. They've never had a chance to ski, and they're crazy to try it. What do you charge?"

Mark thought fast. He had never had lessons from a professional himself, but he had taught Elmer and Emily the fundamentals. The best course, he thought, was to be frank about it.

"I'm not a real ski teacher," he said with a grin, "but I'll be glad to give it a try. Why don't you watch how we make out and then pay me whatever you figure it's worth?"

He led the two children up the slope at one side of the main trail, showing them how to use their skis in climbing. When they reached a fairly flat place, a few hundred feet from the bottom, he let them rest. Then he gave them five minutes of level skiing, teaching them to keep their skis parallel and close together, and showing them how to push with the poles.

When they had lost their fear of falling, he started them on downhill work. The slope was gentle, and no turns were needed. Within half an hour the little boy was schussing down with whoops of delight. The girl, more timid at first, finally got enough confidence to follow. And at the end of an hour they were both skiing happily in spite of a few spills.

The man and his wife had been watching anxiously. Now they came over to Mark and shook his hand. "I've tried to teach them," said the father with a smile, "but

I didn't have your patience. This is worth a lot to us. What would you say to five dollars for the hour's instruction?"

"It sounds like too much," Mark told him. "I know that's what the pros charge, but I expect they do it better."

The man laughed. "Results are what count," he replied. "Here, take the five bucks! And we'll probably be back for more."

Before the day ended, Mark had given two more lessons. One was to a high-school girl he knew, and he didn't ask her for any money. The other was a middle-aged businessman from Stroudsburg. He had a poor sense of balance and his coordination was largely lacking, but he seemed determined to learn to ski.

Mark spent a difficult hour with him and felt they had made little progress. Nevertheless, the man was pleased. He paid the five-dollar fee without question and insisted he meant to keep on till he was able to make a decent showing.

When they were counting up the money that night, Mark tossed ten extra dollars into the pot.

"Where'd that come from?" asked Elmer.

"You'd be surprised," his brother said with a chuckle. "Man, you're looking at a real ski pro! From now on I reckon I'll have to change my name to something that sounds Norwegian or Austrian. Never mind—every little bit helps."

Chapter 16

That Christmas was one Mark would never forget. Right up to Christmas Eve the Wilkins family was busy at the ski slope. A little fresh powder snow had been added to the good base, but it fell during the night so that there was no break in the fine skiing conditions.

With Christmas Day coming on a Sunday, Saturday brought the biggest crowds they had ever had at Blueberry Mountain. More than two hundred and fifty skiers paid for tickets that day, and the lunch-counter business was so heavy that it took Mrs. Wilkins, Emily, and Bess to handle it. Mark had to make two trips to the village for extra supplies. And he gave four hours of lessons as well.

Most of the crowd left by midafternoon in order to be home for the Christmas Eve festivities. As dusk settled over the mountain, the weary family counted the profits and found they had taken in more than two hundred dollars.

"I don't think we should even open the place tomorrow," said Mark. "There wouldn't be many coming anyhow, and Buck and Bess want us all at their house for dinner."

They wrapped their small gifts that night, the younger children hung their stockings by the kitchen chimney, and everybody went to bed early.

Christmas morning dawned gray and cloudy with a

threat of snow in the air. Mark's weather studies had told him to expect a new cold front, so he wasn't surprised. After breakfast and the opening of presents, they all walked down the road to the Evanses' house together. Mark stopped at the lodge and turned the sign around to indicate no skiing. A few flakes of snow were beginning to fall, and it was doubtful if any customers would drive up till the weather improved.

Bess was at the door to greet them, looking more radiant than ever. She had on a new dress and was excited about having her family as Christmas guests. But there was something more to her high spirits. It wasn't long before Mark discovered the reason.

Mr. Evans, seated in his wheel chair, took Mrs. Wilkins' hand and held it while he made an announcement.

"You and I and Mother, here," he said, beaming, "are going to have a grandchild, come July. What do you think of that?"

Mark's mother gasped and hugged her daughter, while Buck stood by, looking proud and embarrassed. The young Wilkinses let out a whoop and danced around their sister.

"No baby," Bess said with a laugh, "ever had a wilder bunch of uncles and aunts than mine will."

While the ladies cooked the dinner and the youngsters played parlor games, Mark and his brother-in-law went out to the barn to talk. Buck was positive, of course, that the baby would be a boy.

"Not that I wouldn't like a girl, too," he admitted, "but I want a son to work the berry crop with me an' take over the farm some day."

Mark laughed. "Looking a pretty long way ahead, aren't you?" he asked. "It'll be forty years before you're ready to retire."

They talked about the ski slope, and Mark mentioned

the idea of putting in a tow during the coming summer. "Elmer and I figured we could do it for under fifteen hundred dollars," he said. "If we get a few more weeks o' good skiing, we'll have pretty near that much saved."

"How much do you have in the bank now?" asked Buck.

"Counting the two hundred I got back from Tuttle," Mark replied, "there's right around seven hundred in the account. And I give Mom something every week, besides."

"Keep a good set o' books, so you can show just what your profit is," Buck suggested. "Then, come spring, I'm pretty sure you can borrow all you need from Joe Sullivan at the bank."

Mark nodded. "No harm in trying, anyhow. And if we get a tow running, we can charge more an' make more. There's one other thing I want to plan for later on—a stock o' ski goods. Quite a few people have asked if we carried 'em. But that can wait till the slope's solidly established."

"Right," said Buck. "Don't get overextended at the start. Besides, you'll be away at college, won't you?"

"If I can get in," Mark answered. "It'll either be college or a hitch in the service, so I guess I won't be around to run things next winter. Elmer's growing up, though. What I'd like to do is leave the slope in shape so the family can keep it going."

They went back to the house through the snow, and at two o'clock everybody sat down to a huge dinner. For once, as Mr. Evans remarked, "too many cooks" hadn't spoiled a thing. The party was a great success.

* * *

The snow was light, and it lasted only a few hours. By Monday morning the sky was clear again, and the wind cold from the northwest. The skiers returned in greater numbers than ever.

Among the first to arrive was Clyde Roebuck, the radio

man. He had to be back in town to do his broadcast at six, he explained, so he had spent the night at Mt. Pocono and would be driving back soon after lunch.

"But I wanted to get in another visit here while the snow's so good," he added. "Did you hear what I said about you a couple of weeks ago?"

"Sure did," said Mark. "And thanks! A lot of people have mentioned that plug, and it's kept us jumping since the last big snow. My mother made fresh doughnuts this morning, so you'd better have some while they're still hot."

As they entered the lodge, a station wagon drove up. Mark recognized it and waved to Jean Langley, who had come with a party of friends. A moment later he was proudly introducing her to the sports commentator.

"You really put Blueberry Mountain on the map, Mr. Roebuck," she said with a laugh. "But I discovered it first, didn't I, Mark? By the way, we've opened up the camp at Beaver Lake. Come over and see us some night, won't you?"

He had little opportunity to talk or ski with Jean that day, but she stopped once to watch him while he was giving a lesson. The pupil was a college girl, somewhat timid and awkward on skis.

"May I butt in?" Jean asked with a smile. "I had a ski instructor in the Alps once, and he helped me get over just what you're doing. When you start down the slope, your skis sort of wander, don't they? The tips get farther apart, and you slow down or fall down. Well, I found out I was leaning back too far and holding my knees too stiff. Look, try it this way."

Gracefully, she bent her knees and leaned her body forward from the hips. "See if you can do that," she said. "Do a few knee bends first, till you get a comfortable position. Good! Now, when you hit a steeper slope, all you have to do is bend the knees more, lean forward a little farther, and keep your arms well out in front, like this—see?"

The pupil was less self-conscious with a girl helping her. Within five minutes she had made a creditable schuss and was enjoying it, no longer tense.

"Gee!" Mark told Jean. "What I need is you for a teacher. I couldn't seem to make her loosen up. Look at her now!"

"The woman's touch." Jean laughed. "You're getting to be a genuine pro, aren't you? Giving many lessons?"

"About four or five on a good day. I don't think I do it very well, but they learn somehow. And the money all helps."

"You must be doing pretty well financially," she told him. "Look at all those half dollars! The slope's covered with them!"

"It's paying," he admitted. "Just give us snow and we'll make out fine."

Jean and her party were there several times that week. On Friday evening Mark dressed up, borrowed the pickup, and drove over to Beaver Lake. In the Langley living room he was introduced to the crowd of boys and girls. Soon he took his place in the circle around the log fire. One of the men sitting near him was a Princeton student named Bill Gresham.

"Don't you lead a pretty dull sort of life up here in the backwoods?" he asked Mark with a patronizing smile.

"That depends. We don't get bored very often. There's too much to do. I suppose it isn't what you'd call exciting, though."

"Now wait a minute," Jean put in. "I'm not sure what Bill thinks is exciting, but you might tell him about that ex-convict you caught."

Mark reddened. "There wasn't much to it," he said in embarrassment. "Just a character named Mort Tuttle who

was holed up back on the far side o' the mountain. He'd been jack-lighting deer an' killing 'em out o' season. Then he held me up one night an' took a couple o' hundred dollars—cash I'd made on the ski slope. The state troopers found where he'd driven his jeep into the woods, but they couldn't follow him in—too much snow. I was good an' mad about losing the money, so Buck Evans an' I went over the mountain on snowshoes. We found his cave in a ravine an' took him by surprise."

"Whew!" Gresham whistled. "I take it all back about things being dull up here. Seems to me I read something about the affair in the New York paper. Right after Thanksgiving, wasn't it?"

Mark nodded and hoped the subject would be dropped, but they pressed him for more details. At last he was glad when somebody turned on the record player and they started dancing. It was a pleasant evening, and though Mark had little time alone with Jean, she did take him aside before he left. It was to thank him for the Christmas copy of his father's book and to say how much she had enjoyed it. He went homeward whistling contentedly.

The week between Christmas and New Year's was about over, but they had been blessed with good skiing and excellent business. Even if a thaw came now, Mark knew he would have at least a thousand dollars put away toward the improvements he hoped to make.

Warmer weather and a drizzle of rain spoiled the slope on Saturday and continued over New Year's Day. The following Tuesday the holiday crowd was gone, and the Wilkinses all went back to school. Mark had a book report due a week later, and with his English teacher's permission, he chose his father's novel, *Lift Up Mine Eyes.*

He had heard parts of it read aloud, but this was the first time he had read the book seriously and straight through. It was better than he had realized. Many passages had the rhythm and flow of true poetry. But more than that, the characters seemed alive—poor but friendly mountain people, bearing their troubles with fortitude. He could almost hear his father's quiet voice in some of the sentences he read.

The book was selling fairly well, he knew. And the critics had praised it. Earlier in the fall Jean had sent him a clipping from the *New York Times Book Review,* calling it "a fresh and thought-provoking novel" and expressing sincere regret over its author's death.

Mark worked hard to make his report worthy of the book. He got an "A" on it, which pleased him. Then he was back in the regular routine of school and basketball.

Elmer was playing at least part of every game now, and the two Wilkins brothers made a formidable backcourt combination. The first few games after the holidays were played against schools in their own class. Winning them, one after another, the team was still unbeaten when they journeyed up into the coal regions to play a strong, tough five that had won from them the year before.

It was a battle, all the way. Twice in the last two minutes the score was tied. Then their opponents went ahead on a field goal, matched a moment later when Moose Martin made a fine over-the-shoulder jump shot. In the last five seconds Mark was fouled. He went to the line, closing his ears to the roar of boos from the crowd, and tossed in the winning point. The rest of the squad carried him off the floor on their shoulders.

The string of victories was kept intact right up to the ninth game. Again their big test was to come against Stroudsburg High, a good-sized school that had been winning against tougher competition.

The squad worked hard that week. Good as their record was, Coach Winton had kept them free of overconfidence. On the clear, cold February night when they boarded the bus to go down the mountain for the game, every man was in top physical shape and fired up with the desire to win.

With two unbeaten schools meeting, the contest had drawn a lot of attention. Spectators were coming from all over the northeastern part of Pennsylvania, and because of the big crowd, they would be playing in the spacious field house of the nearby state teacher's college. On their way to the dressing room the Crow Ridge boys got a glimpse of the floor and the many-tiered stands, already beginning to fill with people. It looked vast and forbidding. The coach saw the look of awe on the faces of the squad and laughed.

"Look here," he said. "That court isn't an inch bigger than the ones you've played on all season. Baskets are the same height, too, and both officials are men you've worked with before. All you have to do is play basketball and forget how many people are watching you."

Mark knew the words made sense, but he still had a feeling of insignificance when they filed out on the floor for pre-game practice. It wasn't helped any by the appearance of the Stroudsburg squad. Where, he asked himself, had they dug up so many giants? He kept on shooting doggedly, but out of the corner of his eye he could see a tall, graceful figure lobbing them in at the other end of the floor. That must be Clipper Ferrand, often mentioned as an all-state prospect. He played forward, and Mark was sure he would be assigned to guard him.

Ten minutes later he was shaking hands with the celebrity. Ferrand wasn't quite as big as he had looked—six-three or so—but he still loomed over Mark. And he had a careless smile that showed he wasn't in the least nervous. At the whistle he moved a stride to his right, reached above Mark's head to take the tap from his center, and was off down the floor with easy speed. Mark had to put on a real sprint to get between him and the basket.

In the corner, fifteen or twenty feet out, Ferrand bounced the ball with a tantalizing grin, glanced left as if to pass it out, then jumped with a twisting motion and fired an effortless one-hander through the cords. The roar of applause didn't penetrate Mark's consciousness. He was angry at himself as he took the ball at the base line and tossed it out to Chuck Wagner. That, he told himself through gritted teeth, was the last time Mr. Ferrand would fool him with a head fake.

Chapter 17

The first ten minutes of that game were like a nightmare. Off to an early lead, the home team was able to relax and enjoy it. They were having a hot streak. It seemed to Mark that every shot they made flew toward the basket as if drawn by a magnet. Crow Ridge, meanwhile, was too tensed up to play its usual game. Shots rolled on the rim and refused to go through the hoop. Passes went wild and were stolen or fell out of bounds. Even veterans like Moose Martin forgot their assignments. When the score had climbed to 23-7, Coach Winton called a time out.

"Well, boys," he said quietly, as they mopped themselves with towels, "I've seen a few cases o' buck fever, but never one like this. Most o' the time out there you looked as if you'd lost your heads completely. I'm going to let you sit on the bench for a while and see if you can shake off those jitters. Mark, you're staying in because you seem to know what you're doing. Keep that Ferrand guy bottled up. Their shooting's bound to cool off soon, and I hope ours'll get better. All right—report to the scorer's table. Greg's in at center, Elmer Wilkins at the other guard, Bud Lee and Ferd Johnson at forwards."

The second-stringers went in with fire in their eyes. They figured the situation couldn't get any worse, and perhaps they could make it better. Mark passed out to Elmer, took the ball again to cross the center line, and caught the enemy napping with a quick flip to Greg Martin. The youngster unlimbered his long legs, jumped high, and dunked a two-pointer through the cords.

Stroudsburg's happy fans laughed and cheered at the effort, still confident of a lopsided victory. Their guards brought the ball out lazily, lobbing passes back and forth while they waited for the forwards to get positioned. Ferd Johnson, sticking closely to his man, saw a low bounce pass coming and darted out to grab it. His toss to Bud Lee was on target. Fast-breaking down the floor, three Crow Ridge players and the two Stroudsburg guards reached the keyhole almost together. Lee passed off to Elmer Wilkins, who shot from a dozen feet out with an opposing player hacking at his arm. The ball went in, and he followed it up by making his penalty shot. The last five points had all been scored by the little team from up the mountain.

Mark was sticking to Ferrand like a leech. Several times he was able to block the star's shots or force him to pass off to a teammate. But Ferrand was too good to be stopped entirely. Before the half ended, he had made two more field goals. Crow Ridge, meanwhile, was steadily closing the gap. When the teams went off the floor, the score stood at 30 to 22.

The four regulars who had been benched surrounded the subs in the dressing room. They slapped them on the back and gave them full credit for making a game of it.

"But gee, Coach!" Moose Martin pleaded. "Give *us* a chance now. The kids have shown us how to do it, an' we're rarin' to go!"

"You'll get in all right," Winton replied. "But don't think it'll be easy the rest o' the way. We had 'em off balance in those last few minutes, an' that's the only reason we began to outscore 'em. You've had your breather. Now let's go out there an' shoot some practice goals."

Eagerly the squad ran out on the floor, yelling encouragement to each other as they took their shots. This time Mark didn't even notice when the other team appeared. He was too busy sharpening his eye and his timing. Once more it was the Crow Ridge varsity that started the second half.

He could feel a tremendous difference in the way his teammates played. Everyone went at top speed, passing cleanly, waiting for the right second to shoot. Big Moose was rebounding like a fiend under the basket. Twice he outjumped the tall Stroudsburg center to recover the ball off the backboard, and on both occasions his alert forwards were able to score.

After each two-pointer the Crow Ridge boys went into an all-court press. It seemed to rattle their opponents. Some of the passing grew erratic, and once Ferrand, trying to dribble past Mark's close guarding, was called for too many steps. His supercilious smile was no longer in evidence. With five minutes gone, he had added only one field goal to his total, and the score had crept closer. It was 40 to 38.

Worried, the Stroudsburg coach called time, and when his team returned to the floor, there were two new faces in the line-up. Winton was content to stay with his regulars. It was several minutes later that Mark tied the score with a long, arching two-hand set shot from nearly thirty feet out. When the figures went up on the board—44 to 44—there was a shrill cheer from the faithful little band of Crow Ridge rooters. What had looked like a slaughter had turned into a hard-fought battle that could go either way.

The Stroudsburg forwards began hitting again, but the boys from up the mountain matched them, goal for goal. The two-minute warning came with the bigger team ahead by the margin of a single point.

Elmer Wilkins came in once more at guard, and Mark, tired as he was, felt a fresh surge of confidence when his brother joined him in the backcourt. Stroudsburg had the ball. From the cautious way they moved it down, Mark sensed that they had orders to freeze it.

"Stay right with your man, kid," he told Elmer. "Don't foul, but get that ball."

The seconds ticked off on the clock. At the end of half a minute their opponents were still dribbling carefully and making short passes that couldn't be intercepted. Nobody seemed to have any intention of shooting. Then Mark realized that Ferrand was edging toward his favorite corner. There was a crafty look in the big forward's eye. Sooner or later he meant to take a shot that would clinch the game.

Mark thought fast. He backed off a step and let his arms droop as if in weariness. The strategy worked. As soon as the Stroudsburg guard who had the ball caught sight of him, he flipped across toward the star forward. And the instant the ball left his hand, Mark was moving. He sprang in front of Ferrand, saw the ball coming, and went up with all the spring he could put in his legs. His outstretched fingers just touched the leather, but it was enough to deflect the course of the pass. A dozen feet away Joe Rossi took the ball as it hit the floor and dribbled out of reach of a frantic Stroudsburg player. Elmer was going down-court like a scared rabbit. He took Joe's long pass over his shoulder, jumped for the hoop, and laid the ball up for a clean two-pointer.

There was less than a minute left, and now it was Crow Ridge's turn to protect a one-point lead. Their opponents were looking for another all-court press, but to their surprise the mountain boys let them bring the ball across the mid-line without interference. Then the close guarding began again. Mark and his teammates

CROWRIDG
44
TROUDSBURG
21

knew they couldn't afford to foul, but they were determined to block anything that looked like a shot.

Both sides were watching the clock. Tension mounted in the big crowd, and the constant yelling was enough to deafen a man. Finally, with only a dozen seconds to go, Ferrand cut past Mark, shoving him off with his elbow, and aimed a one-hander at the basket. It hit the backboard, hung for a breathless moment on the rim, and fell off into a swarm of reaching hands. It was Moose who got it. He squirmed loose from the crush of players, dribbled toward the corner, and let fly with a fifty-foot pass down the floor. Mark caught it on the dead run. He bounced the ball once and looked back at the clock. The game was won now. All he had to do was freeze it for four short seconds. But the basket looked too tempting. He fired from where he stood, twenty feet out, and the ball swished through the hoop just as the final whistle blew. They had beaten their rivals by three points—62 to 59.

Mark was the last man back into the dressing room, for he had been stopped and congratulated by many of his friends. The rest of the squad, still in uniform, had gathered around Coach Winton, talking excitedly.

"Hey, Wilkins!" Link Freeman called. "Did you hear the news? We had some college scouts watchin' us!"

"So?" asked Mark, pulling off his jersey and getting ready for a shower. "Who were they?"

"I don't know for sure, but I heard there was a guy from Temple an' one from Villanova—both big basketball schools."

Mark shrugged. "Probably here to see Ferrand," he said. "You'd better hustle or I'll use all the hot water."

He thought no more about it until they were in the bus. Then Winton came and sat beside him. "You played a mighty good game," said the coach. "Kept their star bottled up and did your own share of scoring besides. Have you picked a college you'd like to go to?"

Mark turned and looked at him. "I'd thought of Penn State, if I could get in," he answered. "The tuition would be lower, for one thing."

"Suppose you didn't have to worry about tuition," Winton said with a grin. "What would you think of Lafayette, for instance? Their scholastic standards are good, and the campus is only forty miles or so from here. A classmate o' mine, Jim Hunter, is coaching there now, and he saw tonight's game. Seems to think he'd like you on his team. Would you be interested in talking to him?"

Mark took a minute to think it over. He had never been one to overestimate his own ability, and the idea of an athletic scholarship had simply never occurred to him.

"I know Lafayette's a fine school," he said at last. "It sure would be handy, too. Yes, I think I'd like to talk to your friend. Thanks a heap."

"He's got a game tomorrow night," said Winton. "They're playing Colgate, I believe. Why don't you go down there, see the game, and have a word with the coach? I'll give you a note to him."

Mark found it hard to get to sleep that night. The next day was Saturday, but he was up early, finishing the chores and putting on his best clothes. The skiing was good on the slope, but he knew he could safely leave its management to the rest of the family. At noon he boarded a bus in Mt. Pocono, bound for Easton.

Where the highway led down the hill past the college campus, Mark got off. For an hour or two he wandered among the buildings, looked at the stadium and the gymnasium. Then he went to the coach's house and rang the bell.

An attractive young woman came to the door. Evidently she took him for a college student. "Yes?" she said with a smile. "You wanted to see my husband?"

"Yes'm, if he's home," Mark replied. "At least, I've got a note for him from Chip Winton, up at Crow Ridge."

She nodded and led the way to a small room at the back of the house. It had been fitted up as a den.

"Jim," she said, "this young man has a letter from your friend, Chip Winton. Can you talk to him now?"

The lanky redhead sitting at the desk stood up and grinned. "Sure can!" he answered. "You're Mark Wilkins, aren't you? Come in and sit down."

He gave the note a quick reading, then nodded. "I watched that game last night," he said. "Crow Ridge seemed to have the collywobbles there, at first. I liked the way you helped pull 'em out of it. Also the way you handled that Ferrand lad."

He paused, laughing. "To tell the truth," he went on, "I'd gone up there to take a look at him, but I hear he's got a bid from one of the big southern universities. Anyhow, what I'm really looking for is a good backcourt man who can start the plays, steady the team, and do a bit of scoring on his own. Have you decided where you want to go to college?"

"Not yet," said Mark. "I'd sort of considered Penn State, to save on tuition."

"How are your school grades?" Hunter asked.

"Mostly A's with a couple of B's," Mark told him. "I took my preliminary College Boards last spring an' did all right."

The coach looked pleased. "We have a few athletic scholarships here," he said. "They're fairly modest, but enough to take care of the tuition. I think I could get you a part-time job that would cover room and board, if you'd like to come to Lafayette. Of course, you'd have to keep up in your studies."

He laid a freckled hand on Mark's knee. "Don't try to make up your mind too fast," he said. "Come to the game tonight and meet some of the boys on the squad. Then I'll get you a bed at a fraternity house, and you can go home tomorrow."

"I'd like to see the game, all right," said Mark. "But if I can catch a bus after it's over, I'd better get back. The folks might get worried."

It was just after midnight when he reached Mt. Pocono. By luck he saw a Crow Ridge boy just getting into his car to go home, and Mark hitched a ride with him. They talked about the game he had seen in Easton.

"Lafayette looked mighty good beating Colgate," he said. "I've got a hunch they may get a bid to one o' the big tournaments next month. Their coach thinks so, anyhow."

He tiptoed into the house and up to his room. Quiet as he had been, Elmer was awake.

"Hey," whispered the younger boy excitedly. "What happened down there? Are you goin' to Lafayette?"

"You ought to be asleep," Mark told him. "Nothing's settled yet, an' I don't have to decide for a few days, but I guess they'll take me if I want. How was business today?"

"Pretty good," said Elmer. "Didn't break any records, but we took in better'n a hundred dollars. A couple o' folks wanted lessons, an' I told 'em you'd be back tomorrow."

"Good." Mark yawned. "Now turn over an' keep quiet. I've got to get some sleep."

Chapter 18

The sky was gray with a threat of snow the next morning. Even so, a good many skiers were on hand at the slope, and Mark was kept busy while the rest of the family went to church. At noon Moose Martin came in and gave him a hand with the lunch service until Emily and her mother showed up. Then the two boys went up for a run over the trail. Mark had said nothing about his trip to Easton, but somehow the word had gotten around.

"Hear you're goin' to play basketball for Lafayette," said Moose with a grin.

"I might," Mark replied. "Matter o' fact I'd take the offer in a minute if you were going to be there, too. How about it? The coach seems like a good guy, an' he's a friend o' Chip Winton's. You an' I've always worked well together. I bet they could use you on the football team, too."

But Moose shook his head. "What I want's an agricultural course," he said. "Either Cornell or Penn State. Pa wants to build up our dairy herd, an' I need to study animal husbandry."

They came zipping down the slope and shot over the bump at the bottom like a couple of soaring birds. A man who wanted ski lessons was waiting for Mark when he pulled up beside the lodge. He worked hard until three-thirty, and then the snow began to fall. The skiers started to leave. After the last car had pulled out, he went down the road to the Evans house.

Bess and Buck were in their apartment, which they had fixed up on the second floor of the farmhouse. They welcomed him warmly as always and wanted to hear all about the Stroudsburg game. From that, Mark plunged at once into his problem. When he finished, he asked their advice.

"Sounds like a first-class offer," said Buck. "If I were in your place, I'd take it."

"But," Bess put in, "you aren't going to college just to play basketball. What do you plan to study? What would you like to do for a living afterward?"

"That's just it," Mark replied. "I'm not cut out for science or engineering. Maybe I'd like to be a writer, like Pa was. There are good jobs in advertising if you can really write. So I reckon what I need is a liberal-arts course, majoring in English. Lafayette would be just the ticket for that."

"You might get in a course or two in business administration," said Buck. "If you build up the ski slope, put in your tow, an' start selling equipment, you'll have a business that'll support the family while you're in college. And at Easton you'd be near enough to get home and run things weekends whenever the skiing's good."

Mark nodded. "That's one o' the angles I'd thought about," he said. "I haven't talked to Mom yet, but I'm pretty sure she'll agree. If you both think it's a good idea, I'll write to Mr. Hunter and accept. Now I'd better hike for home before this snow gets any deeper."

His discussion with his mother went about as he had expected. She was anxious for her children to have good educations, and this seemed a fine opportunity for Mark. He wrote to Jim Hunter in Easton and mailed the letter next day.

Occasional fresh snows kept the skiing good well into March. Meanwhile, the basketball team finished the regular season and went down to Allentown for the first round of the regionals. The fact that they were beaten in a close game was no disgrace. The team that defeated them moved on to the state finals and won the Pennsylvania championship.

A week later Mark heard from the Director of Athletics at Lafayette. If he passed his College Entrance exams with good marks, he would be accepted and receive an athletic scholarship.

Immediately he buckled down to his books. That month he studied harder than ever before in his life, but the work paid off. When his third-quarter grades came in, he had four A's, one A-minus, and one B. He thought he did almost as well in the College Board tests. Then Easter vacation arrived, and he could devote his time to the ski slope with a clear conscience.

Another timely snowfall had put the mountain trail in top condition. Over the first vacation weekend they averaged better than two hundred customers a day, and the money mounted up fast. Under a new system he had worked out, all the cash taken in for refreshments went to his mother for housekeeping expenses. The admissions, less what he spent for supplies, were saved up toward improvements on the slope. The only money Mark kept for himself was what he made from ski lessons. This would buy clothes and give him a start in Easton.

Day after day he watched for the Langley station wagon, but Jean didn't appear. He had written her, telling about his college plans, and received no answer. At last, on the final Saturday before school reopened, he saw Mr. and Mrs. Langley drive into the parking space. He welcomed them at the cabin door.

Mrs. Langley was friendly, as always. "It's such nice

winter weather up here," she said, "we thought we'd just have to come for one weekend. Jean's away in Canada."

Seeing the disappointment in Mark's eyes, she went on quickly. "One of her school friends invited a party up to Mont Tremblant for the holidays," she explained. "Of course the skiing is wonderful there. The only thing Jean didn't like was that she'd miss seeing you."

Mark smiled again. "Gee, she's lucky!" he replied. "I guess Mont Tremblant's got the finest slopes anywhere east of Aspen or Sun Valley. And she's such a swell skier, she'll get the most out of it."

A week later he got a letter from Jean herself, and any hurt he had felt was gone. She described the crisp, cold air of the Laurentians and the marvelous trails she had skied. There had been parties around the big log fires at night, where she had met a lot of nice young people. But her interest in Mark seemed as warm as ever. She was delighted to hear about the athletic scholarship, and she finished by saying she would see him as soon as she could come up to the lake after school was over.

April brought warm weather and showers that washed away the snow. The skiing was ended until winter came again, but Mark was well satisfied. He went over the accounts and totaled up the profits from the slope. With all bills paid, he had a net of $1,186 to show for the season.

During the noon hour next day, he walked over to the Crow Ridge Bank and Trust building. Back of a glass partition he could see Joe Sullivan seated at the cashier's desk. At the moment he wasn't busy, so Mark pushed open the swinging gate and entered. Time had been kind to the lame boy Mark remembered. He was still short and slightly built, and when he stood up, as he did now, his limp was obvious. But he wore well-tailored clothes and looked like the successful banker he had become.

An engaging grin spread over his Irish face. "Well," he said, "if it isn't little Buddy Wilkins, grown up to man's size! Buck said he thought you might be dropping in. Here—have a chair."

They shook hands and Mark sat down. "I'd like to get a business loan," he said, coming right to the point. "It's to make some improvements on our Blueberry Mountain Ski Slope. Have you seen the place?"

Sullivan nodded. "I drove up by there at Easter time," he said. "Looked like a busy place. How do you plan to improve it?"

Mark outlined the idea for a rope tow. "Elmer and I can do most o' the work," he explained. "We figure all the materials and a good second-hand engine can be bought for under fifteen hundred dollars. There's better than eleven hundred here in the bank now. What I'd like to borrow is another five hundred. If you'd like to see our balance sheet, I've brought it along."

The cashier went over the neat columns of figures with a practiced eye. "You've done a good job with what a lot of people thought was worthless land," he commented. "Made a pretty nice profit this winter. Do you plan to charge more when the tow's been installed?"

"Yes," Mark answered. "A dollar shouldn't be too much for a full day's skiing. And I know quite a few new folks'll come if they don't have to climb the trail. It means they can make at least twice as many downhill runs."

"Let's see," said Sullivan. "I suppose your taxes are all paid up, and you own the property free and clear. The tax rate may be increased since you've made improvements, but not a great deal. It all looks like a sound business to me, and I can authorize a five-hundred-dollar loan without bothering the directors. How soon do you want it?"

"Not for a few months, anyhow," Mark told him. "The

later I get it, the less time I'll have to pay interest. I figure the money we've got will take care of everything but the engine, and that doesn't have to be put in before fall."

With their business out of the way, they talked about basketball and college. Joe Sullivan highly approved of Mark's going to Lafayette.

"I'm on the Selective Service Board," he said. "Your name came up the other day, and I told 'em you were the head of a good-sized family. So you can go to Easton without any worry about being called up. There'll be time enough for your hitch after you've finished college."

* * *

A lot of things happened that spring. As soon as the weather warmed up, Mark worked every evening and weekend, helping Buck add new acres to the blueberry patch. When the ground was cleared and plowed and harrowed, they transplanted hundreds of little green bushes from the cold frames. Then there was the usual spring work on the older part of the plantation.

April 25 was a memorable date, for on that day a check arrived from the publishers of Elmer Wilkins' novel. The statement showed a sale, up to the end of December, of 22,000 copies. And the royalties, after taking out the $2,000 advance, came to the startling total of $7,900! It was far more than any of the family had expected, and it gave Mark a feeling of security he had never known before. He could go off to college in the fall with the assurance that his mother had plenty of money.

She wanted him to use some of it on the tow project, instead of borrowing, but he steadfastly refused. There were other things she needed more, and the responsibility for the slope was his own. Besides, he knew it was good business to establish his credit at the bank.

Finally, as May drew to a close, Mark had a chance to begin work on the tow. He laid it out with care. Starting well to the left of the cabin, he marked the line with a row of stakes. The slope on that side was fairly even, and he chose the spots to set his poles in ground that was free from rocks or ledges. There would be twelve poles in all, two hundred feet apart.

Elmer, meanwhile, had been up in the woods behind their house, picking out trees. As soon as Mark could join him, they took their axes and a crosscut saw and felled a dozen good, straight hemlocks, each at least eighteen inches through at the butt. Lopping off the branches and peeling the bark with spuds required several days' work. When it was finished at last, they hitched chains around the poles and hauled them out, two or three at a time, with Buck's tractor.

Each pole was about thirty feet long. "They don't have to be too tall," Mark told his brother. "Just high enough to keep the rope clear o' the snow. I figure twenty or twenty-five feet o' pole above ground ought to be plenty."

The weather had turned hot by the time they were ready to dig the holes. Mark had foreseen that this would be the hardest part of the job, but it turned out even worse than he expected. They worked a whole Saturday morning on the first one, taking turns at the digging. At a depth of four feet they ran into loose rocks that had to be pried out with picks and crowbars. Elmer lost interest about that time. He was really too young to have the strength and endurance that were needed. Mark didn't bawl him out for quitting. He just wiped his sweating face, spit on his hands, and went on shoveling.

After a hurried lunch he went back to tackle the second hole. Here he encountered a solid ledge a foot below the surface. Fortunately, by shifting his location a yard or so uphill, he found softer going and was able to finish before suppertime. His hands were blistered, and he knew his muscles would be sore in the morning, but the idea of giving up never crossed his mind.

Buck came to the slope after church the next day and

helped him dig the third hole. When they got through, Buck was panting. "Whew!" he said. "I wouldn't trade jobs with you for a lot o' money! But outside of hiring a utility line crew and a mechanical digger, I guess there's no other way to do it. More power to you, boy!"

Every evening that week, rain or shine, Mark toiled at the project. Sometimes he worked till it was dark as pitch in the bottom of the hole. Once or twice he had to stand ankle-deep in water while thunder rolled overhead. By Friday night he had only four more to go, and on Saturday Elmer came back to help him.

"Here," said the younger boy sheepishly, "I can't stand to see you kill yourself. Gimme that shovel."

At dusk, Sunday evening, they completed the final hole. Mark straightened his back and mopped his brow. "Golly, what a job!" he breathed. "I never worked that hard in my life. Sure hope it's going to be worth it."

They had to postpone further labor until after graduation. Mark, with the second-highest standing in the class, was slated to be salutatorian, and he worked over his speech night after night. Meanwhile, final examinations were held, and there followed the class picnic, the senior prom, and other less formal festivities. Commencement was later than usual that year. It didn't come until the twenty-third of June. The day dawned bright and clear, and though the mountain air was cool in the morning, it promised to be hot by midafternoon.

At two o'clock Buck came in his car to pick up the Wilkins family. Bess was with him, looking a bit uncomfortable in her maternity dress, but she smiled at Mark as he climbed in.

"I know I look a sight," she said, "but I wouldn't miss seeing my little brother graduate for anything!"

Chapter 19

Mark was still whispering the opening lines of his salutatory address as the procession climbed the steps of the open-air platform. Because it was such a fine day, it had been decided to hold the exercises outside on the big lawn. Close to a thousand people—relatives, friends, and students—had gathered for the occasion. There weren't enough chairs to hold them all, so some were seated on the grass or were standing under the trees.

After an opening prayer, the speaker of the day took his place on the podium. He was minister of a big New York church and spent his summers at Beaver Lake. Instead of giving them the usual long-winded oration, he spoke for only about twenty minutes, and his words were wise, witty, and to the point.

With the applause still ringing in his ears, Mark suddenly heard his own name spoken. He was being introduced. With the awful feeling that he had forgotten all he meant to say, he got stiffly to his feet and crossed the platform in front of his classmates.

"Friends," he began, "neighbors, parents, and fellow students, it is my privilege to greet you on behalf of the graduating class of Crow Ridge Consolidated High School."

Somehow the words seemed to come of themselves as he stared out over the audience. He could even pick out the proud, intent faces of his mother and his brothers and sisters in the throng. Everything went beautifully until he reached the closing remarks. Then his eyes lighted on a figure at the rear of the crowd. It was Jean Langley. He stumbled over a word, recovered, and went on. The last few lines were delivered in a fine, ringing voice that he could hardly believe was his own.

The applause when he finished was more than polite. There were even a few spontaneous cheers as a tribute to his popularity. With a deep sense of relief, he went back to his seat and the program continued. At last, one by one as their names were called out, they got their diplomas and left the platform to mingle with the crowd.

While Mark was still being embraced by his family, Jean pushed her way through to his side.

"Well, look who's here," said Mrs. Wilkins with a smile. "What do you think of our boy orator, Jean?"

The girl looked at Mark shyly. "I thought it was pretty wonderful," she answered. "But then, I've found he does a lot of things well."

"I never figured you'd be here," Mark told her. "When's your own graduation?"

"Oh, I beat you to it." She laughed. "I got my diploma last week, and now we're up here for the summer. The water's still a little cold, but a few days like this should fix it. Why don't you come over for a swim some day?"

"I'd like to, all right," he said. "But there'll be a lot for me to do these next few weeks. Berries are ripening, an' that keeps us all on the jump. Still, I'll try to get over there soon."

With the big day over, Mark got back into dungarees and went to work. The berry crop was bigger than ever. From daybreak till dark the Wilkins family picked and sorted and packed. Buck and Mark took turns hauling berries to the freezer and selling them at the cottages around Beaver Lake. With more fruit to dispose of, Buck decided to expand his route to other mountain resorts. The single pickup truck was no longer adequate.

"Tell you what," he suggested to Mark. "I'll go halves with you on a used car. The extra sales we make ought to pay me back, an' the car'll be yours at the end o' the summer."

They went together to a dealer in Stroudsburg and purchased a three-year-old station wagon that was in good mechanical condition. There was almost as much room in the back as in the pickup, so their deliveries were practically doubled.

Mrs. Wilkins had insisted that Mark's share of the purchase price should come out of the family bank account, and he agreed on one condition. That was that in September the car should belong to her. He wouldn't need it at college and could travel back and forth by bus.

The big event of that July was the birth of Bess's baby. It was a fine, big, healthy boy, and Buck was so proud that he wore a constant grin and walked with a strut. To Mark's surprise and delight, they decided to name the baby after him—Mark Wilkins Evans. The first time he held the fat little pink-and-white bundle in his arms, it gave him a strange, choked-up feeling.

When the rush of the early berry season was over, there was more time to work on the tow. By the end of the month, with the help of Buck and Elmer, Mark had set all twelve poles, filled stones in the holes around them, and tamped the earth in solidly.

The crossarms were six-by-four timbers, each about fifteen feet long. They had been mortised and bolted to the poles while they were still on the ground. Meanwhile, an order for the rope, carrier wheels, and other hardware had been sent off to the mail-order house. But nothing in the catalog seemed to be suitable for the big pulleys around which the rope would have to run at the top and bottom of the tow. Worrying over this problem, Mark discarded several plans and then went to talk it over with the blacksmith in Crow Ridge. The man was more than just a horseshoer. He was a practical workman in iron.

"Yep," he told Mark. "I can see what you're after, an' I reckon the bigger the pulleys are, the better. How about that old pair o' wagon wheels back o' the shop? They're good stout oak—no loose spokes—an' the rims are strong. I could take extra-wide iron tire stock an' shape it with a flange on each side, so the rope wouldn't slip off. How do you figure to keep just the right tension on your rope?"

"I don't know exactly," said Mark. "That was one thing that was bothering me. If I set the engine in concrete, a mile o' rope is bound to stretch or shrink with the weather, an' it might get too slack."

The blacksmith nodded. "Reckon I can fix that for you, too. You'll have a vertical shaft with the wheel mounted on it—right? Why not put the whole thing on a pair o' tracks, so you can move it in or out? I could fix you a couple of iron dogs that would hold it fast any place you wanted it."

"That sounds like the perfect answer," Mark agreed with enthusiasm. "How much do you think such a rig would cost me?"

"Not too much. 'Course, you'd have to build a platform, maybe three foot high, for the tracks—to keep 'em above snow level, that is. You get that done an' buy your engine, an' I reckon I can tend to the rest. The whole business shouldn't come to more'n sixty bucks."

Cheered by this news, Mark went to the lumberyard and bought heavy planking and posts for his platform. He paid a litle extra for having them treated with creosote to resist rot and weather. Then, back at the slope, he and Elmer went to work. Six more holes had to be dug for the posts, but this time they were only two and a half feet deep. Mark lined each one with old boards, mixed a batch of concrete, and poured it in around the bottoms of the posts while his brother held them straight.

"We'll wait a day for 'em to set," he told Elmer, "an' then saw off the tops an' make 'em level before we lay the sills."

"Gosh," said Elmer, "you're sure building a long platform. Twenty feet! Why's it have to be that big?"

Mark laughed at him. "You ever notice Mom's clothesline in the back yard?" he asked. "On a good clear day it hangs loose. Then along comes damp weather or rain, an' the line tightens up. What do you think would happen to forty-eight hundred feet o' rope? We have to give ourselves room to take up the slack or let it out."

With the platform built, Mark set out to look for an engine. At Buck's suggestion he went to see a tractor dealer, down near the Wind Gap. What he needed, he explained to the salesman, was a heavy-duty engine, not too high in horsepower but sturdy and dependable.

They looked at a number of used tractor engines, some nearly new, others rusty with neglect. Finally he chose a rugged-looking thirty-five-horsepower engine that seemed to have had careful use. When he told the dealer that it would be geared to a vertical shaft, the man produced some transmission and clutch parts that might be helpful. In all, Mark paid him three hundred and ninety dollars.

It was Joe Rossi, Mark's teammate on the basketball squad, who helped him set up the engine and driving apparatus. Joe's father owned a garage, and Joe had grown up working around cars and trucks. First he tuned up the motor and made sure it ran smoothly. Then he put in a clutch and fitted a bevel gear to the end of the engine drive shaft. It meshed with a larger gear attached to the bottom of the upright shaft that would drive the rope wheel. It was about as simple as any transmission could be. They built a little housing of sheet metal to protect it from the weather and bolted the whole assembly to a sturdy carriage made of three-inch planks.

Several days later the blacksmith arrived in his battered old truck. He looked over the engine and the job the boys had done in setting it up. "That ought to work fine," he said with a nod of approval. "Here's the two cart wheels an' the track I've fixed up, an' I brought along four little flanged wheels from an old mine car to run on the track. I see you've got the platform finished, too. O.K., just leave me be now, an' when you come back, we'll have everything running."

The man kept his promise. After a few hours Mark returned to see him pushing the engine carriage back and forth along the platform tracks. On the head of the vertical shaft sat one of the wagon wheels. Its iron tire had an inch-deep flange on either side.

"Now take a look at these dogs," said the blacksmith, pointing to two wedge-shaped pieces of iron hinged to the bottom of the carriage. "They'll dig in an' hold anywhere you want her, an' she won't creep."

* * *

Two more weeks passed before the shipment from the mail-order house arrived. Mark got a card saying he could pick it up at the Lackawanna freight depot in Mt. Pocono. Knowing the rope would be heavy and bulky, he borrowed the pickup and had Elmer follow in the station wagon. But when he got there, the sight dismayed him. There seemed to be a veritable mountain of bright new manila hemp piled there on the platform.

He had ordered the rope in twelve-hundred-foot lengths —the longest he could buy—and there were four immense coils of it, each weighing close to four hundred pounds. With the help of Elmer and the stationmaster, he managed to get two reels into the truck and a third one into the rear of the wagon. Another trip had to be made to pick up the last coil of rope and the hardware. Buck suggested that everything be left in the Evans barn for the time being.

"You know," he said, "my father served a hitch in the Navy once when he was young. That rope has to be spliced so it'll run smooth over the carrier wheels, an' Dad's probably the best splicer on the mountain. It'll make him happy, too—give him something he can do."

The crop of later blueberries had ripened now, and the whole clan was working overtime. Usually Mr. Evans felt left out of things at such times, but now he, too, had a job. In his wheel chair he sat at the open doorway of the barn and used a marlinespike with deft sailor's fingers. The splices he made in joining the lengths of rope were real works of art. When Mark came in to see how the

job was going, the invalid invited him to shut his eyes and run a hand along the rope. So tight and smoothly fashioned was the splice that he could barely tell when his fingers came to it.

"That," said Mr. Evans proudly, "would take a thousand pounds o' pull an' never let go."

He spent nearly a day on each splice, and when he had finished, he suggested another task for himself. "This rope's going to be outdoors all winter," he said. "It'll take quite a beating from the weather. To stand up, even for a few seasons, it ought to be tarred. That'll give it a better grip on the wheels, too. If you'll get me the tar, I'd like to put it on myself."

Mark knew he was right, though the idea of applying the sticky stuff hadn't appealed to him. "Are you sure, Mr. Evans?" he said "Don't you mind getting all messed up?"

The older man chuckled. "To tell you the truth," he replied, "I love the smell. Makes me think o' ships an' the sea. No, I'll enjoy every minute of it."

* * *

Mark had kept up the interest on his bank loan, paying it each month out of the wages he received from Buck. With a decent amount of snow next winter and the tow in operation, he knew he would be able to pay off the loan without trouble.

Using a ladder, he and Elmer had mounted the carrier wheels on the outer ends of the crossarms. All that remained now was to string the rope, and there was no hurry about that.

As soon as the rush of work in the berry patch eased off in August, Mark had time for a visit to Beaver Lake. He put his swim trunks in the car and drove over one Saturday morning. Jean, he was relieved to find, was at home and had no other dates.

They walked together along a trail that led back through the deep woods. Once, in a little open glade, they saw a doe and her half-grown fawn. Deer were strictly protected in the forest around the lake, and these were so tame that they merely trotted away when they heard the hikers' voices.

"Boy, it's pretty here!" said Mark. "I don't wonder you come back year after year."

Returning to the cottage, they had a swim before lunch, played some records, and danced a little. After they had eaten, Mark invited Jean to ride over to Blueberry Mountain with him. He wanted her to see what he had done with the tow.

"Why," she said, looking up the slope at the row of sturdy poles, "it's all so professional! I can't wait to see it running."

Mark laughed. "Let's just hope it does run," he told

her. "If you're here for the first good skiing weekend, we'll find out."

"Wild horses couldn't keep me away," she said. "I'll be here—that's a promise."

Chapter 20

In September, before the first frost reddened the mountain maples, Mark left for college. It was all pretty strange at first. He found he was no longer an important figure, as he had been at Crow Ridge. He was just one of four or five hundred bewildered freshmen, wandering forlornly around the campus. He had to wear a "beanie" and obey the rules laid down by the upperclassmen. The restrictions irked him, but he had the good sense to do as he was told and take the mild hazing without losing his temper.

He was more fortunate than some of the other first-year men. Jim Hunter, the basketball coach, kept a friendly eye on him and helped him get off on the right foot. His quarters in the freshman dormitory were nothing fancy, but he liked his roommate, a quiet, studious boy from New Jersey named Don Hall.

To help pay his way, he had two jobs. One was waiting on table. It wasn't heavy work, and there was nothing to be ashamed of in doing it. That took care of his board. The other task, which paid ten dollars a week toward his room, was shelving books in the library. It was something he could do in about an hour each evening, and it didn't interfere with his study time.

Since he was carrying a fairly stiff schedule, he spent

more time on his books than he ever had in high school. An hour or two of touch football, between classes and supper, gave him enough exercise to keep in shape.

Hunter had advised against his going out for the regular freshman football squad. "Too many chances of getting hurt," he said. "I want you to report for basketball in good condition when we start practice in November."

Saturday afternoons he sat in the rooting section and cheered the maroon-jerseyed Leopards on to victory. And every second or third weekend he got home to Blueberry Mountain.

After many days of happy labor, Mr. Evans had finished tarring the rope. In addition, he had attached hand lines at fifty-foot intervals along its whole length. One Saturday in late October, when Lafayette was playing a game away from home, Mark decided it was time to complete the tow. He enlisted the help of Elmer, Buck, and several neighbors, and they loaded the rope into a hay wagon, hauled by the tractor. First, they passed a loop of it around the cart wheel at the foot. Then, moving slowly up the hill, they draped the strands over one pair of carrier wheels after another.

Mark had been worrying. He was afraid he would find the rope too long and have to shorten it, or too short, requiring him to move the platform. As they neared the top, he eyed the coil of tarred manila still in the wagon and shook his head.

"She'll never make it," he told Buck. "I guess I set that last post too far up."

"No, sir!" said his brother-in-law stoutly. "I'm betting on a miracle."

They pulled out the final loops of the rope and were still a dozen feet short of the post that held the upper cart wheel.

"Look," said Buck. "Down below it's sagging 'most to

the ground between some o' the poles. If we all get hold an' pull, I think we'll come out about right."

Five of them hauled on the big line, but it was too heavy for them. Then Buck uncoupled the tractor, threw a loop of rope over the winch, and drove slowly up the last rise, picking up the slack. All working together, they manhandled the rope around the flanged wheel and stood back to admire the result. To Mark's astonishment, it turned out to be an almost perfect fit.

"Yippee!" he yelled in relief. "Let's get down there an' start her up!"

With Elmer he raced headlong down the half-mile slope. There was gas in the tank, and the old tractor engine started without difficulty. Slowly Mark eased in the clutch, and the gears began to turn. The rope creaked on the big homemade pulley. It didn't slip. It was moving! At four or five miles an hour it went up the hill, made the turn at the upper pulley, and came back.

By the time the rope had made a full circuit, Buck had brought the Cat down. He grinned and shook Mark's hand.

"Looks like your tow's in business!" he said.

* * *

Well before Thanksgiving, Mark found himself adjusted to the college routine. He had to work a bit harder than some of the boys from bigger schools, but he was able to keep up with them in his classes. He didn't court popularity, and it came to him as a surprise when he was elected secretary of the freshman class. Some of his themes in English composition had received good marks, and his friends knew he could write.

"You're just the guy to handle the minutes of class meetings," his roommate told him.

Meanwhile, basketball workouts had started. Mark had expected to be far behind the experienced veterans on the squad, but he discovered he could run, pass, and shoot with almost any of them. All he lacked was size, and that didn't worry him too much. He was still growing. On the measuring platform in the gym he now stood at an even six feet.

After two weeks of practice he was picked as floor captain of the freshman team. The yearlings would be playing a schedule of only six or seven games, but in daily workouts they were used against the varsity. In some of these sessions they held the older men almost even, and Coach Hunter was pleased.

"You're doing all I hoped for," he told Mark. "With another season's polish, you ought to be ready for the varsity starting five. And I understand you're keeping your grades up. Fine! Stick with it, boy!"

Don Hall had a radio he had brought from home, and Mark listened to the weather forecasts with close attention. A cold front that headed east in late November held some promise of snow for Thanksgiving. On Tuesday night Mark hurried back from his chores in the dining hall and turned the dial to Clyde Roebuck's station.

"Hi, there, fellow skiers!" the commentator greeted his audience. "Got some good news for you tonight. It's been snowing up in the Poconos since noon. Six inches on the slopes already, I'm told. If this keeps up, you and I can look forward to some fancy schussing over the holiday. I haven't heard from young Mark Wilkins, but I expect he's got a tow working at his Blueberry Mountain layout this winter. Anyhow, as I've mentioned before, that's a good fast trail, and Mark's mother makes the best doughnuts and coffee you ever tasted. Of course, if you're looking for something a bit swankier, I can recommend a trip to Sky-Top or Baird's Notch. And still farther away, you'll find excellent skiing now in New York State and New England."

Mark turned it off at that point. "Hey!" Don exclaimed,

looking up from his book. "Was that you he was talking about? I knew you liked to ski, but what's this about your own slope?"

"That's right." Mark laughed. "It's just a little old country ski trail we fixed up. We were lucky, though. Clyde Roebuck came up an' liked the place. He gives us a plug once in a while."

Others must have heard the broadcast, too. Within half an hour a dozen students came to the room, kidding Mark and asking how to get to Blueberry Mountain. Then the telephone rang at the end of the hall. Another freshman answered it and yelled for Wilkins at the top of his voice. Mark hurried out and picked up the receiver.

"Hello," he said. "This is Mark Wilkins."

"The famous Mr. Wilkins that runs the ski slope?" asked a familiar voice. "Hi, Mark! In case you hadn't guessed, this is Jean. I just wanted to tell you I'll be keeping my promise. Dad and Mother have agreed to drive up with me for a Pocono Thanksgiving. Is it really snowing up there?"

"All I know is what I hear on the radio," Mark told her. "Not much has fallen yet here in Easton, but the weather looks promising. Anyhow, I'll have the slope all prettied up for you. Maybe a surprise, too."

"Good!" She laughed. "I'll see you Thursday."

One of the things Mark's mother had done with the money from the book was to have a telephone installed. He called her that evening and asked to have Elmer meet him at Mt. Pocono with the car next day.

"I've only got one afternoon class," he explained, "and I can afford to cut that. So I'll be on the bus that gets there at three. How's the weather up your way?"

"Lots of snow," she told him. "That ought to make you happy, and Elmer's put chains on the rear wheels, so I guess he can get through."

The sun was out Wednesday afternoon, and the hills were beautifully white along the highway as the bus moved up into the higher country. Where the street had been plowed in Mt. Pocono, the banks of snow stood shoulder-high along the curb. Elmer was there to pick up his brother.

"Hi, big shot!" he said with a grin. "Wait till you see the ski slope. It's just about perfect."

They stopped at the lodge, and Mark whistled with surprise. He hadn't been home for three weeks, and in that time a tight little shed had been built over the engine.

"Golly!" he exclaimed. "That's a relief. I'd been worrying because it wasn't covered. Who did the job?"

"I put her together," Elmer admitted. "Used old lumber we had left over. Got it done just in time, too."

Mark gave him a grin of appreciation. "You're getting to be quite a responsible guy," he said. "Must be you're growing up."

The whole family was awake before dawn on Thanksgiving morning. The boys did the barn chores together and set off for the slope immediately after breakfast. Elmer and his mother had laid in supplies for the lunch counter. They lighted the range and the heater to warm up the cabin, then went out to start up the engine. After a dozen tries it sparked, chugged once or twice, and finally settled to a steady rumble. When the clutch was let in, the rope slipped at first, for it was stiff with ice. Mark got a grip on it with his mittened hands and pulled until it started into creaking motion. Within five minutes the tow was working smoothly.

"She's stretched since we rigged her," said Mark, sighting up along the carrier poles. "Better pull the carriage back a little."

They stopped the engine, held the carriage with a crowbar while the dogs were loosened, then pried it back until some of the slack was taken up.

"There," Mark panted. "That ought to do it. Now let's start her up again and try the tow."

Quickly they put on their skis. Then each of them grabbed a hand line, and in a moment they were moving smoothly up the snow-covered slope.

"Hey!" called Elmer. "This sure beats climbing, doesn't it?"

The knotted lines that hung from the rope were long enough to let them keep their grip, even at the high points where the rope passed over the pulleys. Mark had been expecting trouble, for it seemed impossible his homemade rig wouldn't have some bugs in it. But no difficulties developed. They reached the top, turned, and took off down the unmarked trail.

By ten o'clock the first customers arrived. Nobody seemed to object to the increased price of a dollar,

especially since there was no charge for using the tow. Mark kept a watchful eye on the rig. He knew the real test would come when fifteen or twenty skiers were being hauled up at one time. The engine strained and panted once or twice but didn't stall under the load. At noon he stopped it long enough to refill the gasoline tank and oil the bearings. In the interval most of the crowd jammed into the lodge to get warm and eat a fast snack. Mrs. Wilkins stood beaming behind the counter, watching her doughnuts melt away like snow in April.

"Don't eat too many yourselves," she warned little Bill and Janie. "We're having turkey and all the fixings tonight."

Just as Mark was starting the engine again, he saw the Langleys drive in. Jean put on her skis and came over to greet him. Her face was radiant as she looked up at the smoothly running tow.

"Aren't you proud, Mark?" she said. "I think it's pretty

wonderful, myself. It seems such a little while ago that we first came down that slope, dodging the stumps!"

"Two years," he told her with a grin. "Come on—this thing'll run all right without me, and I want you to try it out."

They let the tow take them the first half mile, then climbed the rest of the way to the head of the trail. From that point they could look out across miles of snowy hills bright in the winter sun. But Mark couldn't take his eyes off Jean. She seemed more grown-up, he thought, but prettier than ever.

"How's college?" he asked.

"Fine," she said with a laugh, "though I'm working like a dog. Bryn Mawr isn't easy, you know. Tell me about yourself."

"Well," he said, "I think I'm making the grade. Not just in basketball, either. I mean—I'm doing some writing. Not very good yet, but my stuff's improving. They even accepted some short verse I wrote for the college magazine."

He paused, red-faced. "Please, Jean," he said, "don't think I'm bragging. I just want you to know about a dream I've got."

She took his arm and squeezed it. "Go on, Mark," she said. "I understand."

"This slope is part of it," he told her. "Year by year I want to improve it. I want to build a bigger lodge, for one thing. Then there's room for another trail over there—with more turns. And I'd like to start a ski shop where we can sell equipment. By the time I graduate, the place ought to give me a pretty fair income, and the beauty of it is that most of my time will be my own. I can write or study or even travel. And I can live right here in the Poconos. Does it sound silly to you?"

"It sounds great," she said, her eyes shining. "And if I know you, Mark, you'll make all of it come true."

"O.K.," he said with a laugh. "As long as you believe in me, I can't miss. Let's go! I'll beat you to the lodge!"

They dug in with the poles and were off down the mountainside, as free as a pair of swooping hawks.

www.ingramcontent.com/pod-product-compliance
Lightning Source LLC
Chambersburg PA
CBHW020549310726
48979CB00008B/1145/J
9781931177788